Against All Enemies
Part 1: Troublemaker

Anthony Paul

Cadmus Publishing
www.cadmuspublishing.com

Acknowledgements

First thank you to my Creator for allowing my existence on this earth. For giving me the hand to write and the will to do so and the mindset to accomplish all that I set before me. I want to say to thank you to my Mother for always being there and believing in me and choosing to have me. I want to thank my Brother's and Sister for being there and for who they are, Brandon, Lee, Christina. For my wonderful Daughters Roxie and Rain. To Amanda and Nevaeh for the understanding. To all my fans and followers who have the belief in me to bring them real pain and happiness at the same time. To Sam for being who you are and believing. Shout out to my homies lockdown and in the struggle who fuck with me because I'm 100!! House, Fry, Fruit, Glo, Juice, Ri and Ham, to all my peoples lockdown only you can hold yourself back and not accomplish what you set out to do. RIP to my Pops Paulie and Uncle David and Nikki and my Grandma, as long as I live so do you. Big shout to my Bro from another mother Ace Jonez, thank you for the chance to be on the label and do the music and books with you. You gave me a hand when no one else was trying to and I thank you for that. I get out we taking over real talk, I love you Bro. Music Legacy Entertainment for LIFE!!! Follow us on IG at and get the music and spread the word. To my ppl Colleen, Marla, Mc, Vicki, Clancy and Chad.. Hickory stand up and MLE for LIFE. Thank you to Cadmus and your support.

Table of Contents

PROLOGUE

Pablo walks out into the cold night and lets the rain wash away the blood. He looks up to the dark sky and thinks about the holes that have been punched into his heart. Then he lets his anxious mind also replay the day his Pops told him a very vital truth to survival in the streets. "Be cautious of all those you entertain or allow to be inside your circle. Anyone at anytime can or could be a threat. Just as the book of Micah chapter 7, 'everyone lies in wait to shed blood; they hunt each other with nets. Both hands are skilled in doing evil; the ruler demands gifts; the judge accepts bribes; the powerful dictate what they desire-they all conspire together. Do not trust a neighbor; put no confidence in a friend. Even with the woman who lies in your embrace, guard the word of your lips. For a son dishonors his father, a daughter rises up against her mother; a daughter-in-law against her mother-in-law, a man's enemies are the members of his own household. Do not gloat over me, my enemy! Though I have fallen, I will rise. Though I sit in darkness, the Lord will be my light."

CHAPTER ONE

C hica just make sure that you're parked outside waiting. 13 and a wake up." Pablo says to Alejandra before placing the phone back inside its cradle on the wall. Pablo then heads outside in front of C building to meet up with his homeboys. Convicts and inmates stand around smoking whatever they desire to with no regard for the officers or the prison rules. The one common thread is its us vs them. If you're not on that same wave you cannot be on the compound. You ride out in the box. Isolation. You have wolves and sheep. Play that beast role you better be able to hold your own with your hands, feet, locks, 190, or knives.

Pablo has on the designed khaki pants, white tee, issued by the prison. The Jordan 3's that are on his feet are not. Keeping any sort of contraband shows that the convict can hold his own, he's not a snitch, he has respect from both sides. Pablo stands at 5'9", 162lbs, solid muscle, bald fade, tatted from his neck to his ankles.

He's mixed with Black, Mexican, Irish, Cherokee, German, and white, so his skin is a light coffee hue. He has 13 days left on a 5 year sentence for robbery and a pistol. Alexis Martinez, his teenage love, best friend, and lawyer handled the plea for him.

His girlfriend Alejandra Inez Lopez will be out front to pick him up from this modern-day plantation. They have known each other since they were younger. The last 5 years Alejandra has been the one holding him down here. Helped his family as well, however possible. As he steps onto the big rec yard he clears all thoughts of the outside. All the people on the other side have once again gotten subconsciously buried. Once Pablo reaches where his homeboys Tony, Slimm, RedBalla, and Tomas are lined up on the chain linked fence, backed by razor wire 3 fences across and all around. Gun towers, roving check trucks, and 3 correction officers on the rec yard with at least 400-500 caged men.

Pablo daps up each of his homeboys. "What's good?" Slimm, Tomas, Tony, and RedBalla reciprocate with bumping fists and saying they are good and like always strapped up. Strapped up is one or more weapons that range from ice picks to bonecrushers, which are named so for this very reason. The bonecrusher will be short as a forearm to as long as an arm and it will crush any piece of the body it touches. Then there are the homemade vests, some are newspapers, most are magazines, and the best are hardback books.

As on cue all five of them place a folded towel around their neck. You learn fast in prison, especially a close custody/medium prison to protect every piece of your body and the vital ones that you care to protect at all cost. Prison is not a boxing ring or MMA cage.

"Check it, once this shit pops don't stop until you're cuffed and hauled to the box." Pablo looks at each of them and their eyes have changed from man to beast.

"Just don't forget me when you leave in a couple. that's all of you." Slimm answers. He has 20 more years to go on a 45 year sentence for killing his sister's husband. Respect-in prison is different than in the world.

"Just hit Angelica up for that lick, it's all set and ready to go." Tomas says to Pablo.

"'Balla, we going to set this Detonator off on this bomb." Pablo says. "I'm cool wit dat. Know I appreciate the love you all have shown me from day one." RedBalla tells each of them.

He's a OG Piru from Cali that caught a case in the great state of North Carolina. The thing is he came in on man time, ten down, front line, and has been Pablo's bunkmate for the last 2 years.

"They posted and ready too. I want Rolo bitch ass. Nobody touch him." Tony speaks as he is tightening his boot laces.

"CC," "CC," "CC," "CC," "Piru!"

They all 5 move as one onto the grassy track that leads around the rec yard. Pablo and RedBalla are side-by-side as Tony, Tomas and Slimm follow. Pablo's eyes move everywhere watching and as their walking it starts going silent. Silence is a deadly prelude to violence. Silence in any environment is a warning to everyone. Pablo thinks that comes from the beginning of creation.

"They are on the move." Slimm states, nodding his head getting ready for the bloodshed that is about to commence.

"Sangre por sangre." Tomas says aloud in Spanish.

"Dawg. You sho' 'bout this? You touch in two weeks." Red-Balla asks Pablo in a low whisper.

"No doubt. My shawty and fam know how I rock. Shid you ain't got but a year left. You ain't gotta be here, yet it's about loyalty. About respect."

"Say less."

About 10 yards in front of them is a group of other convicts and a couple inmates. Their flunkies. When any type of disrespect is shown you have two choices, in their mind and 95% of others you actually only have one. Bake a cake and blow out the candle. Settle it right there on the spot, or become known as weak. Then there is the choice of gathering your clique, homeboys, whoever you rock with and set it off. This is not their problem, it's Tony's, he allowed a Mexican to disrespect him. He's cliqued up with the Southsiders. Tony was playing spades in his unit and didn't know the dude was slick disrespecting him in Spanish until another Spanish dude told him. This happened last night, retold at breakfast and now here they are in the rec yard in a standoff. Ten yards apart. Dirty Harry style.

"Remember on my cue." Pablo says to RedBalla.

"Are you positive about hitting him? Y'all was cool."

"Yep. I don't do this for no award, it's off GP and loyalty." Pablo is or was cool with the rep for the Southsiders until a couple weeks ago. On visit Bony slicked eyed Alejandra and when Pablo asked him about it, he rolled his eyes and said his bad. Pablo right then decided to pop his lid before leaving. This shit with Tony only sped it up.

Pablo takes two steps and stops to show he'll talk to Bony if he desires to do so. Bony steps up and stops, they both meet in the middle. No dap, handshake, nods, nothing. Silence before it's broken by Bony. "So this what it comes to? It was all fun, my homie meant no disrespect." Everyone in the system knows a lot of Mexicans are racist towards Blacks. "Let them shoot one." Pablo tells him, meaning one-on-one.

"No es uno pelar con hermano. Es morano, tu es loco." Bony speaks in Spanish to let his homies know what Pablo wants. Pablo already has the scene played out in his mind.

"That's how you want to play it? Cool. Too much pride gets a man hurt. A good General knows when to war and when not to." Pablo rubs the top of his head and at the same time shit erupts on the other side of the rec yard. Code detonated. Two shines are double teaming an MS-13 and that in turn sets off the C.O. 's radios. Concussion grenades being thrown from the gun towers on the two corners of the rec yard. At the same time Pablo grabbed his 6 inch shank before Bony could respond he started stabbing him in the face.

This in turn starts Slimm, RedBalla, Tomas, and Tony to rush and start stabbing anything in their sight. An all out riot has erupted on the rec yard between the Blacks and Mexicans. The Puerto Ricans, Dominicans, and a couple Colombians are backing the blacks. The white gang members are backing the Mexicans. The inmates who aren't involved or attempting to get involved are getting out of the way and laying down on the ground. Half excited, the other half scared. Pablo lays Bony down and sees Slimm going at it with three Mexicans and an Aryan and goes to his aid. Slimm is leaking and Pablo is also but they get back to back and start putting in the work. Pablo is wrecking shit Red-Balla and Tomas are standing over Tony who is laid out on the ground with a pick in his eye.

"Shots will be fired! Get down! 5 4 3 2 1!"

Boc! Boc! Boc!

Boom! Boom!

More concussion grenades, the SERT team is all out in full gear breaking and wrecking the rec yard. The first shots are almost always rubber bullets. Pablo takes a shot to his right leg that folds him at the same time he is hit with the riot shock shield. He loses consciousness. "Casey all I need is a couple minutes. Five tops and this is the last request I make." Pablo asks the slim white C.O.

"You're right, it is for now. Imma do it only because you're leaving in less than an hour. Don't come back, if I see you again, let it be out there."

"Thank you. You definitely will not see me on this side again. Fuck this plantation and the powers that be. You just protect your pretty self and keep with the real ones and don't switch up." Pablo grabs the property he's taken to the house. Pictures, mail, and a couple books. Then he snatches up the small laundry bag to take to RedBalla. "I'm ready."

Casey, the majority of the population call officer or Ms. Mox, unlocks the trapslot to the isolation cell Pablo has been in for the last two weeks. Now they're walking down A range and Pablo speaks to a few comrades and tells them to hold it in the road. They step off A range and walk the short hallway to D range. Tony, still in a coma, the ice pick only took out his left eye. The trauma to his head is what has him laid up fighting for his life.

Casey pops RedBallas trap slot on the cell door. "Five minutes max and I got to cuff you also. You know the rules, I'll be standing over here." She walks off about 10 ft or so. Pablo and the rest of their crew became alright with Casey on a humble. Respect in prison goes a long way especially with female officers. One thing that 99% of the convicts, the real men, hate is a gunner. Jacker. Sniper.

Someone who mentally rapes a woman is just like a rapist, child molester, only one rung away from the scum. So on a day about a year ago, Casey was working the hallway door to the mess hall. When a perv pulled on his meat, his dick through a hole in his pocket he was not only violating her. He was disrespecting everyone in line who could see the action. RedBalla swung, due to being in line in front of the dude. Then you had the other four jump in and the five of them stomped and stuck him twice for a shit bag. The perv lived even though they wish it would have turned out different. That warranted each of them 120 days in the box and more respect from the otherside. Especially Casey Mox.

Pablo pushes the laundry bag through the hog slot. "It's been real dawg when you touch, reach. All my shit except mail, law work, pictures, and a couple of books are 1n your property. This is the stuff I had over there. No homo, Imma miss y'all. Its fucked about Slimm." RedBalla bends down and Pablo follows so their faces are at the hog slot. "Already. Bra, you my nigga and anytime you need me or any assistance reach out. You know my book straight and I'm about to be ghost also. Slimm went too hard, I've been thinking he did that shit on purpose. I hope Tony pulls through anyway. Imma hold it down and see you on the opposite side one day. Watch everyone and always maintain your serenity, humbleness, most of all your truth." They dap each other and stand up with the last fist bump to the tiny plexiglass window. Pablo moves down the corridor and Casey locks the hog slot back. When she reaches Pablo he places his hands behind him to be cuffed. In the box you're cuffed whenever moving outside the isolation cell. As Casey cuffs his wrists together he is thinking about Slimm.

Slimm went rampage on one of the SERT officers and from the word that got sent was they shot Slimm dead in his face. This is the fucked up reality in prison. Slimm was one of those dudes who felt he had nothing to gain or lose with the time the judge gave him. Prison will sometimes break the strongest men with time inside her walls.

When Pablo walks out of the prison gates he doesn't glance back. Alejandra is running straight at him from her parked black on black Ford Focus. She leaps at the last second and he catches her spinning her around before setting her back down. He unleashes a kiss so soul wrenching God can feel their love.

"I missed you so much! I love you baby! Welcome home!" They're walking and reach her car and Pablo pins her up against her door. "I love you Shawtie forever and a day." He's kissing her and gripping her thick ass. He stops, "Come on before I break that pussy in this parking lot!"

They get into her car with him relaxing in the passenger seat smoking a blunt of Kush. Everything feels different, looks different, the air even smells different. Alejandra doesn't speak, she knows that right now is the time her man is thinking and gathering his thoughts. The silence does not bother Pablo at all he learned at an early age silence is a weapon. The creator gave us two ears for a reason.

Alejandro lives for the moment in a two bedroom bottom row apartment. It's in Hilltop. One room is for her office work, the other her bedroom. She's 24, 5'5", 125 lb, with a body shaped like Cardi B. Full blooded Mexican, originally from Mexico City. She came to the states at 9 years old to live with her mom after the cartel gunned down her father, grandfather, and both uncles. The way she held Pablo down during his stay on the plantation has shown love, trust, and honesty. Most of all loyalty and Pablo has never shit in the face of his Blessing and he cherishes their relationship. When they pull into Hilltop she parks in her regular spot Pablo sees Carlos, Mario, BB, and a dude he doesn't know. They're all sitting around a gray metal El Camino. "Who's that other dude with them?"

"I know his name is Joey and he hooked up with Carlos' sister, Juanita." When they get out of the Focus, Pablo speaks to all of them and pulls BB aside. "What's up Dawg? Yaboy home now and we are fixing to do the damn thing. What's up with your Pops?"

"I'm happy you're out and know it's CC to the grave. Pops said he'll be in touch and to thank you. I don't know exactly what. I know you are ready to start trouble and get money." BB looks like Pablo, the only difference is build and Pablo is tatted up.

"You know it and I got some official plays lined up. I got to catch up with Ryan ASAP. Now he is booming the weed and he got some new shit out the A called Urkle Purple." Pablo starts walking toward Alejandra's apartment with his sandbox friend next to him.

"I heard that it's 10x more potent than the white darkness. We can surely stack cakes as tall as birthday cakes with that."

"Look, I'ma 'bout to go wreck Shawtie back. Be ready to move when I hit you up. We're gonna get together later and chill. Peace."

"Alright. I'll catch you later on over at your peeps house." They dap each other with a half embrace the way men do to other men.

Pablo walks in and finds Alejandra in the bedroom and they collide tearing each other's clothes off. This is their first time together in her apartment. Not in a rush between vending machines or greasing the palms of dirty pigs. No loud noises, no kids running around in the background, silence.

"Hold up, chica! Your man, your king needs something to crush that box too!"

Alejandro lays back on her queen size bed and starts playing with her swollen clit and pinching her thick brown nipples. "Hurry up, daddy! I need that dick and I need it now! You know it's my Nyquil!" She moans and arches her back in pleasure.

"I definitely got you and you're my main course and sweet dessert! I'm going to eat that kitty like I just got rescued as a starving hostage!" Pablo cuts on the stereo system that has Bose speakers all around the room. Out comes the voice of Trick Daddy on 'Tonight' "See good fucking a bring da freak out y'all but if you eat it and don't get cheated then first stuff beat the brakes off her." Pablo rhymes right along with the Mayor of not just Miami, yet thugs everywhere before planting a light kiss on the bottom of her right foot.

CHAPTER TWO

Pablo and BB are sitting in front of the Alltel store on Morganton Boulevard in Lenoir. They're in a stolen Chevy Impala. Gloves cover their hands with matching all black outfits. Their black t-shirts are long sleeve, black polo jeans, with black Air Nikes. Pablo places his two 9 mm on his waistband as he reaches into the backseat. He grabs two of the four Nike duffle bags. "You ready dawg? Shawtie that give me the intel on the spot, told me it's sweet to go no changes." Pablo starts to get out of the stolen car while he relaxes his breathing. Breathe in. Breathe out.

"I was born ready and I'm not thinking twice to bloody anyone up in there." BB has a mini Tech 9 with an extendo and he grabs the other two Nike duffle bags and follows Pablo into the one-story phone shop. It's the size of a convenience store.

As soon as they step all the way in you can hear a pin drop. "Lay down or get put down like a mutt at the vet!" BB screams out. The two blonde haired women can't be a day over twenty, drop straight to the carpeted floor. Soon as they're down Pablo rushes into the office that's off to the left. BB starts filling duffle bags with cell phones. When Pablo is in the office the petite Cuban female that was on her way out, backs up screaming as the 9 comes up point blank Range with her cute face.

"Bitch! Shut da fuck up! Make another sound and your most intimate thoughts will meet air particles! Open the safe and quick!"

The female does exactly as she is told and pops open the safe. She then backs up, cowering and down in the corner. She has her hands over her mouth shedding crocodile tears. Pablo pulls out the blue bank bag, all the loose cash that's kept to run the shop. He reaches one handed in to the duffle he carried into the office with him. He then zips it closed and tells a cowering female, "Look, stay right there and count at least 2,000 before you move."

He turns around and leaves the office and the two blondes are laying still as statues. BB comes from out the back with the first duffle bag loaded. He snatches up the other empty one as Pablo snatches up the other one. They move in silence as they fill up the last two duffel bags and run out the door to the stolen Impala. They tossed the duffels into the back seat and noticed the surfer looking guy staring from his parked car next to them.

"I'm going to pop his top for a Heavenly surf today!" BB shouts as he starts to jump back out of the car.

Pablo grabs his arm applying pressure, "Nah dawg! He's innocent and you know they're off-limits unless need be! Come on!" Pablo drops the car in reverse before BB can even get his body all the way back into the car.

"Damn! Don't drag me dawg!" BB swings into the passenger seat up riding his body slamming the passenger door. Pablo allows silence to envelop the car and calm his racing adrenaline before speaking to BB.

"Look, now this little lick is the start of doing what we've been planning since the sandbox. You have to learn to control yourself. Think rationally, every move has to be correct and not a backward play." Pablo says this as he swerves in and out the lanes to get out of Lenoir as fast as possible. BB doesn't speak, he lights up to two pre-rolled white owls with that good bubblegum redberry inside passing one over to Pablo.

After he smoked half of his bunt he tells Pablo, "You know I know you right. No dick riding, yet you always be on point. The thing and difference is anybody, anywhere, anyplace can get licked like a stripper in the strip club. I have nothing to lose."

Pablo keeps the truth, as always as he speaks his next words. "You do have a lot to lose, starting with your life. Yeah, your Pops is who he is, yet these young animals don't give a shit about that nowadays. I stay on point to stay ahead of all my enemies. The thing is when you start stacking cash and getting proper climbing up the rungs on the ladder they come. So you have to play chess and move with respect to get respect." Pablo inhales more smoke to massage his lungs as he gives BB time to soak up the jewels.

After finishing his blunt BB tells Pablo, "You know dawg I can't disagree with none of that. You can't argue against the truth. It's just I feel we came out of the mud. Either they are with us on the Carolina Cartel or they are in the way and it's no time for fenced strattlers."

Pablo reaches Burke County and the abandoned church lot where is 91 Toyota Cecilia is parked. The paint job is arctic white with carbon flash metallic. The inside is black deluxe, the system is all fosgate. The tires are racing Goodyear Tires with factory rims. The car looks the same as it was before he was sent to prison. His brother, Trip, kept it right.

"We're gonna head over to Shawtie's crib who put me onto that robbery, so we can divide the spoils. After that I'll drop you off wherever. I want you to understand how I feel about what you were speaking about. The thing is we can agree to disagree. We came out of the mud, yet know that everyone can not be in our circle. You know I take loyalty seriously and refuse to be back in the or on the plantation. So, if we keep our circle and CC the correct and proper way, we don't have to worry about others."

"I feel that and I'll either have Tracy scoop me or get you to drop me off. So are you coming out tonight or not? I know it's not your thing, yet we should celebrate. Your home, our pockets getting alright again, and Pops wanting to talk to you about something." He asks Pablo as they get the duffel bags transferred to the Celica.

Pablo responds, "I'll let you know after we finish talking and counting." They both get into the car and Pablo pulls out the abandoned church lot.

"You haven't been uptown to the new joint everyone is going to. It's the spot I told you about over the phone."

"Later about that dawg. First things first."

"That's $14,283 right there, how many phones y'all count?" Pablo has the bills of money in front of him on the coffee table.

"I counted 85." The Cuban girl answers, the one from the phone place.

"I got 153, together that's 238 phones. At $50 a pop that totals $11,900, all together we struck for $26,183." BB says to Pablo. He always had a way with numbers. Probably could teach a thing or two to NASA. BB was a little shocked when they first stepped inside the double wide in Town and Country. Pablo explained that his homeboy on state hooked him up with the Cuban female. Her name is Angelica, BB more than likely won't see her again.

"Check it, we gonna split everything between us, you give Shawtie what you feel is cool. I'm gonna give two bands and nineteen phones. You just make sure you take care of Tomas."

"I definitely will do that and you give me whatever you feel. Pablo I appreciate it and trust all is good. My two coworkers are probably still in shock and don't have any idea about any of this situation." Angelica tells him. Pablo hands her the two bands and nineteen phones." Alright. If anything should switch let me know asap."

"Here's a thousand and nineteen phones." BB passes her pulling on the blunt their smoking.

"That's straight. I'm not tripping, after all I had the easiest part of the job."

With this said and done Pablo grabs up the duffel with his one hundred phones and pocketing his 5,000 dollars. BB grabs up his duffel with his one hundred phones and tells Angelica, "Can you dispose of those for us?" Pointing at the two empty duffel bags. She just nods to not let the blunt smoke escape her lungs. Pablo is headed toward Nuway Circle to drop BB off at Tracy's house. As he's driving he texts Alejandra to let her know he will see her in a couple hours. Pablo passes the blunt to BB as Kevin Gates "Plug Daughter" is slowly coming out the car speakers. "That's the shit I'm tryna to get on. Your Pops has the super plug and we should dump the phones to him at $40 and together. Cop, cook, cut, bag, and slang that Dora."

"I agree, what if he won't take the phones? The Dora isn't the issue, but remember we turned down that offer before. So we should find our own plug who won't think we are looking for a handout."

"If he doesn't want the phones then we push them all over surrounding counties. And if you remember correctly at the time it was all about stealing cars, robbing, and playing with guns." He accepts the blunt back from BB. BB lights a Newport, "Why you wanting to jump in the drug game now? We are almost 26 and you know once in that game it's only really two ways out."

Pablo is thinking to himself about every response from BB as well as his answers. He answers BB with, "Shit, as if robbing shit or shooting it out cowboy style any fucking different. Dawg you acting scared! Real shit. I'm looking at the quickest way to make it out of these streets. Plus with your Pops we ain't got shit to fucking lose!"

BB answers just as aggressive, "Nigga ain't no bitch in my blood! It's just simpler to pull robberies. I-"

Pablo cuts him off, "Look, fuck this back and forth like hoes. Tell him to hallar at me or not. I'm doing this for me and mine."

The next five minutes neither of them speak. When Pablo pulls in front of Tracy's trailer BB speaks first, "I will relay your message and I'm with the move. If we're gonna do it then we gonna do it bigger and better. Cool?"

"Dawg you know we're cool, I ain't understanding your reluctance though. Something I should be told?"

"Nah. Six months to a year run and then I'm out of the drug game no matter what. Cool? We gotta be and stay on the same page to succeed."

Pablo daps up BB and tells him, "Cool with me and I'll put up at CC's later." BB grabs his duffel and tells Pablo as he is exiting the car, "Bet that. Stay alert dawg."

As he pulls off from Tracy's he texts Alejandra to let her know that he is on the way. He stops by Food Lion and quick collects Tomas $200 and then calls Tameka.

"Hello." Tameka answers on the third ring.

"What's good sis? I'm about to stop by to drop something off for the homie."

"Okay. I'll be here when you arrive."

Pablo hangs up, his homie ButterStreetz got indicted for a capital murder charge a few days before he was released. ButterStreetz helped and made sure Alejandra and his family were good all the way while he was locked up. It's only right and real to do the same for his comrade in the arms of the struggle. Pablo and ButterStreetz are closer than BB and him even though all three are cool. Yet, Pablo knows they only truly got along because of him. Still all three have stood ten with each other over the years. Pablo also knows BB is jealous that he's third in command not second.

CHAPTER THREE

S hit! Shit! Shit!" Pablo says aloud while pulling over onto the shoulder of HWY 321. Lucky he has a hidden compartment for his two 9's. He holds his cell in his hand as he awaits the approaching officer.

"Tap. Tap. Tap."

He rolls the window down to look into none other than Detective Johnson's face. "What'd I do today, detective?"

"Nothing Mr. Valdez. I just wanted to say hello and that I hope you learned your lesson. If not, well then we'll be seeing each other. So, my advice-"

Pablo cuts him off with disrespect, "Is that a muthafucking threat? Wait, maybe you'd like to speak with my lawyer Ms. Martinez. I have her on speaker?"

"Detective Johnson, how are we today? Please tell me that you are not harassing my client. If so then I'll be in touch with your superior." Alexis' (Ms. Martinez) voice is loud and clear.

"No mam, there is not a problem, it's a small misunderstanding." Detective Johnson walks off back to his unmarked cruiser faster than he arrived. Pablo pulls off, "Thanks Alexis. I owe you, so what's good?" Pablo asks his closest friend.

"You don't owe me nothing and the same old same. Please just stay outta trouble, you know if given the chance they'll send you back. Or worse, shoot you down. How is everyone?" Alexis asks.

"Everybody cool. I know we haven't really seen each other since I been out. My fault Chica, I'm busy tryna to get right."

"Don't sweat it and just be careful. I have been in court a lot lately, it's as if I forgot what leisure time is." She's laughing along with Pablo and when they settle down she says, "You know I have plenty of money saved-"

"Nah Chica, you keep stacking that bag and soon let me spoil you. Also on that I do need to converse with you on some personal stuff. Just let me know when you have free time. How's your man doing?"

"Well if we ain't got jokes! Know damn well I have no time for a man. Why do you think Benji and I broke up? Speaking of time I gotta meet a client, I'll text you later." Alexis says.

"It's cool Chica, listen though, on the real I need to see you ASAP." Pablo pulls into Hilltop parking next to Alejandra's Focus.

"Agarala Pablo. Más tarde y te amo." She hangs up, as always saying I love you.

Alexis and Pablo grew up together and she wasn't always on the right side of the law. They have a lot of history together that nobody even knows about, not even BB or ButterStreetz. Alexis is a pure 100% Puerto Rican, stands at 5'10", with 125lbs in her frame that sports a B cup and a heart shaped ass. She's hell in the courtroom and will never allow a client to be cheated by the system. It's not about money to her. She got 5 years for Pablo on the Armed Robbery and Pistol charge. The D.A. asked for 15 because someone got shot. The thing was the person kept changing their story, so Pablo got 5 and maxed due to being a troublemaker.

Pablo smiles to himself thinking about Alexis as he walks into the apartment. Alejandra is laying on the couch watching Telemundo. Pablo gives a kiss and tells her, "Let me shower and then we'll grab a bite with the girls."

"Si Papi, I already sent a text to Rebecca to have them ready to go. I'm joining you in the shower." She jumps up off the couch.

"You got it, just know you're coming at your own risk." Pablo says, taking her hand. After spending a few hours with his daughters they dropped them back off at their mothers. They arrive at CC's downtown and it's crowded. BB has a booth in the back that is in a corner and dark. The girl sitting with him he met there. Alejandra is on Pablo's left with BB on his right, the girl on the other end. Pablo has on Polo jeans, black forces, a black Polo tee, with a fitted Panther's hat. The only jewlery is the karat in his left earlobe.

Alejandra has on some Moschino jeans with a matching top. On her size 5 ½ feet is a pair of Sergio Rossi heels. Her jewelry consists of bamboo earrings, a small crucifix around her neck, and a tennis bracelet on her left wrist. BB has an all white Sean John outfit on with low top Forces. He has a Cuban hanging on his neck, a Movado watch, and a karat in his left ear. They're drinking through a bottle of Patron.

BB tells Pablo, "Told you this place be jumping."

"Yeah. It's cool, you know I just don't like the club scene. Just know I made an exception this time. So what did your Pops say?" Pablo is asking this while eyeing two dude's in the opposite corner who he has seen pointing in their direction a couple times already.

"I talked to him at the house and said he'll talk with you very soon. Fuck that for now, let's celebrate and have a good time!" BB takes another drink with his newfound friend.

"Come on Chica, let's get our dance on!" Pablo pulls her onto the dance floor and they move their bodies to "Wild Ride" by Kevin Gates. She's backing her ass up grinding into Pablo's groin causing his manhood to rock up to 1000. Pablo also keeps his eyes on BB and the redbone dancing together, as well as everyone else.

When Pablo pulls Alejandra face to face, an inch apart and moves body to body he raps along staring in her seductive eyes. "Bae you got these niggas jealous/steady wishin they was me/I turned up for a check and got some money off the streets/backseat of the Jag cut up for everyone to see/hit the club next to me!"

They all dance and drink for two hours and decide to leave around 1 a.m. When Pablo sees the two dudes that were in the club pointing earlier. "Yo, who are these two dudes right there?" Pablo nods in their direction.

BB looks and responds with, "Them muthafucka's from over Stonewall Projects. They wanted some burners a few months back, I turned them down and ever since they have been salty. They are just staring scared to jump. Get in." BB tells Redbone as he opens the passenger door to his 98 Cutlass on 22's, cinnamon brown inside and out.

Pablo opens Alejandra's door, "Chica get in while I chop it up with the homie for a minute." Pablo stands with his back to Celica next to BB. "I don't know either of them fools. Now how they was pointing up in there, it just ain't sitting right with me. Come on!"

"Bra wait, it ain't like that, but fuck it! I'm wit' ya!"

As they make their way to the two dudes leaning up on a beat up Seville, Pablo tells BB, "I just want to go be 100 and see what's up. One thing I've learned is that nobody is mugging other men for no reason."

"You know I'm always down for whatever whenever with whoever!"

When they reach the two dudes Pablo sizes them up and can see they aren't a threat. He still looks them in the eyes as he asks, "Y'all seem to wanna talk about something."

The short one who is closest answers with, "BB knows and you should know also. Fuck you CC muthafuckas and this for Ralo!" He swings a razor at Pablo's face, he hits nothing except air. BB rushes and slams the other one into the Seville as Pablo combos the razor swinger. Now it's a crowd gathering as BB and Pablo stomps a mudhole in the two dudes. The only reason they stop is hearing sirens and know they gotta get outta there. They rush back to their cars and leave rubber in the lot.

"Baby you alright? What the fuck was that about!" Alejandra asks, yelling.

"It wasn't about nothing, shit is what it is and calm that ass down."

"I hear you, but you need to learn to chill out. One of these days that attitude and temper gonna lead back down that path. I'm gonna ride or die no matter what, I'm just saying." Alejandra lights and passes him a blunt.

"I hear you and respect it, anyways did you enjoy yourself?"

"Yeah. I just hate the drama that's always there with it."

Before he can answer, his phone starts ringing. He doesn't recognize the number.

"Hello?" He answers.

"¿Cómo está Pablo?" The other voice answers and asks.

"¿Bien? ¿Quién es?"

"Bavil said you needed to see me and that you wanted to talk to me about something that's been on your mind." Rico (El Diablo) Vega answers. This is BB's Pops and he is calling at 1:30 in the morning like it's normal. Business never sleeps.

"Yeah. I It isn't nothing major Tio, just wanted to ask your advice on the upcoming baby shower for Boot's sidekick. Whenever you are ready I'm ready."

"Meet me in one hour at the old kincaid plant on Broyhill Drive. Can you?"

"Yeah I can, I'll be there. Thanks." Pablo hangs up the phone, "Shawtie I got to drop you off and go handle some business. Cool?"

"Yes. Just do what you need to as fast as you're able and be careful."

Pablo pulls into the old plansite on Broyhill as he was instructed to do. The plant is deserted and surrounded by darkness. No one else is there that he can see. He texts a message to Ryan to let him know he'll be out to see him about the weed. When he puts the phone down an all black Denali pulls alongside his Celica. Another one pulls grill to grill, he knows one of them sits El Diablo. Pablo waits and the one in front of his grill opens the front doors with two stocky Mexicans getting out with AR-15's. Then a black dude who has to be at least 7' tall and swole steps out the back right passenger door and waves Pablo out of his car.

When Pablo reaches the Giant, the giant says, "Get in, I'm going to take your car to your house. Where are the keys?"

" Good luck driving and don't scratch my paint." Pablo tosses the keys to the giant as he slides in the Denali. "¿Como está Tio? thanks for the sit down."

"It's nothing. That's what family is for, don't worry about your car. So how has it been since you've been home?" El Diablo asks.

"Everyone is cool, I'm just paddling in the water to stay afloat. I'm trying to get all the way out the sewer to the Superman level. I reached when I did because you know I know you can help me. My situation isn't me asking for a handout. This strictly man-to-man straight level business."

"Straight burn no chase, I like that. Okay. So what is it you want to indulge in? Because you know I have my hands in every basket available on the market. Black or otherwise."

"First off, I have 100 phones and another 100 on Deck. I will take $40 a piece, that's four bands and another four for the others and $4,000 cash. That should be enough for at least a half a brick or a whole brick of Dora."

"What makes you so sure that I need or want 100 or 200 phones? How do you figure that I sell her for that monetary value? What do you even know about Dora?" El Diablo asks as he lights up a Cuban.

Pablo has waited years for this moment, "I don't know if you need any I was fishing. I don't know what your prices for anything are, I'm asking that Is for you to correct me. Now I learned enough in prison about Dora to explore with that broad 4 treasure. So what's up? We walking or just wasting time and money."

El Diablo chuckles, "That's why I've always liked you, your cojones. Tu, corazon, plus you didn't take Bavil down with you. You stood in the paint and carried the weight. You stood up and now it will come back and blessings. Plus you didn't hesitate with that Bony situation. Why do you want to sell drugs?"

Pablo looks at all 5' 10", 250 lb of El Diablo with evilness twinkling in his eyes. "To be real, I learned to be like that from not just the times I was around you. It's Stephen and everyone else. When you have been to the pits of hell and conquered that to make it back into the light, you will snatch anything you want or feel you can succeed from. I know that ain't no money like drug money, that's why. All I need is one year and as far as that other part, loyalty is key to any team."

"What if I told you that there's a game that makes more money than any drug could?"

"I would ask what game and how do I become a player to play?"

El Diablo looks at Pablo and can see it in his eyes, that he wants it for real. Any man that has that look is dangerous and can be used for warrior intent and gain anyone's respect. At the same time never crossed. "Get out and in about 15 minutes someone will appear. One hour after I want your answer and then we will proceed from there. Mas tarde."

Pablo gets out of the Denali and watches as two vehicles leave the deserted plant lot. Wait for what he has no idea, he just knows he is fixing to play. Different mode now, time to reflect and draw out his demon side. He lets his mind wander for a minute and then looks up to the dark sky with no stars. "I told you that I got you."

CHAPTER FOUR

After 15 minutes of waiting an all white SQ4 Maserati pulls in the lot and stops 2 feet from where Pablo is standing. The passenger side window rolls down to show the face of a look-alike Becky G. "Come on and get in, I won't bite." She has pearly white teeth with her fangs encrusted in diamonds. Pablo slides into the seat and she peels off, "Hi, I'm Bianca. You might as well get comfy because we got a long chat coming. Look in the console and light one of those blunts, it's a new strain called Orange Octopus."

Pablo grabs one of the many blunts and lights it, after 2 tokes he is already high. "Damn Shawtie, this da bomb. So, let's talk, I'm Pablo." He passes her the blunt, he scopes her out and she's about 5'1", 125 lbs and rocking the hell out of the Gucci dress with skin that is flawless. Her hair is jet black and gotta be down to her ass. Her right arm is sleeved out with flowers and portraits.

"I know who you are, I know everything that El Diablo told me that I need to on the 15 minute drive to pick you up. I need to let you know up front, I do not fuck nobody that I work with or do any buisness with. Got that?" She passes the blunt back.

"Got it and I wasn't even thinking about it and if you know all about me then it's fair play for me to know about you. Where you from? How old? Etcetera." Pablo pulls on the blunt. "Okay, but nothing too personal. I'm 26, full-blooded Mexican, I'm from Utah originally. I've been working for El Diablo for a year now and I can't complain. The pay is good, is that enough to quell your questions for now?" Bianca asks.

Pablo throws the roach out the window and reclines the seat, "Yeah, that settles it for now. Where are we going and what is this secretive game El Diablo talking about?"

"We just riding right now and let me ask you a couple questions. Just be totally honest, it will stay strictly between us and no answer is wrong. Do you have a qualm about working with a woman?"

"No. As long as said woman knows how to conduct herself and to play her position." Pablo is thinking to himself that if the woman looks like her, he has no problem. Women are God's greatest creation.

"Do you have a problem with taking instructions from a woman?" Bianca lights another blunt.

This bitch can smoke or either she's a nutcase. "No. As long as it consists of getting the job done and not dumb instructions."

"Do you believe a woman can be just as ruthless as a man?" She passes Pablo the blunt.

"It doesn't matter, a woman or a child can be more ruthless than any man given the right circumstances. A woman is more treacherous in my mind." Pablo pulls on the blunt and swears he is surrounded by stars in outer space.

"Okay. Does it matter to you who you murder? Better yet, who can't you murder and why?" She takes the blunt back.

Pablo is so high it takes him a minute to answer. When he does he says, "I'll bust on anybody as long as it's righteous cause or I'm in danger. I don't murder children, that's under 18, I don't kill innocent. Only way I would plant an innocent is if there's no other choice. I only do it if I have to do so because there is no coming back from that. What about you?" Pablo asks.

"I have only killed once and it wasn't a job and don't ask. I just put plans into motion and pass them off, well that is until now. El Diablo told me if you accept that we will be a team, call us BP." Bianca passes the blunt back over.

"Only once and not a job means it was personal. Most murders are like that, well where I'm from and been. So, what does the job consist of? I don't accept nothing less. I know what it is and the stakes." Pablo finishes the blunt and tosses it.

"El Diablo sends me info on certain people who other people take a contract out on, mostly pedophiles. Sometimes just a husband or wife. There is no up, down, left, or right. I get the package and we look at it and do the job. You can't turn no job down."

"So he wants me to be a contract killer, better yet a murder puppet? Can't turn a job down even if I don't agree to it, because that in itself is some bullshit." Pablo doesn't like that part because killing a woman is crazy. Unless she is on some rah rah.

"Look I'm just laying all the cards on the table. Nobody is gonna to force you to do nothing and so far the job has been 99% chomo killings. So that makes a little piece of the world safe. It's your life, your choice." Bianca says.

Pablo thinks for a few minutes and then asks the big question, "How long would by contract be for?"

"2 years, 3 years, it's up to you."

"What is the pay?"

"No less than $30,000, if we fly, bus, train, drive all expenses are paid. When we get to our said destination everything a be lined up. Know that you talk to El Diablo through me on business, you and me stay in contact everyday and when a job comes up you drop whatever you doing at the time."

Pablo thinks for a few minutes before he speaks again, "So it will be just you and me? No one else on these jobs? How many times does a job come down the line?"

"Always just you and me and no one else, we are each other's ears, eyes, smell, heartbeat. Jobs come once a week or 10 a month or more, could be less. So now it's on you to make the choice." Bianca goes silent and lights another blunt.

Pablo is in his own world doing self-talk weighing all the pros and cons. Killing for money is cool, it's like why kill over nothing if you can make 30 bands and 99% of it is ridding the world of sick muthafuckas. Then on top of that, he can kill a muthafucka by torture and test his stomach to the max. He pulls out his phone and texts the words "Si tres anos." to the number that was used earlier when El Diablo first called. Three years won't even be needed, yet the longer the better. He looks over at Bianca, "I'm in, give me your contact info."

They swap info and he takes the blunt from her. This business deal is going to make him a millionaire and help him get out of the struggle. He can also make sure his dawgs that are locked down, can eat and try to bring them home. Plus keep his vow to his Guardian Angel. That's what the majority of homies don't know or understand. You come up you don't look out for everyone, only those who are loyal, real family, if you said that's your nigga then you'll ride or die for that person. That's what Stephen taught him and he will never ever forget that.

"So, where do you want me to drop you off at?" Bianca asks.

"I can chill with you and in the morning you can take me home." Pablo replies, testing her words already.

"Nah. I already told you I don't play where I get paid. So I'm just supposed to drop you off at Alejandra's spot."

"Shawtie I wasn't even thinking on that level, we agreed on that. How do you know about Alejandra or her spot?" Pablo asks.

"El Diablo, that's how, so listen. I will catch up with you tomorrow and hang out just to get to know a little more about each other." Bianca says cutting her eyes off of him to the road.

"Okay with me, I got something to handle in the morning though. So after 12 if that's cool with you boss lady."

"Alright and I'm not the boss, it's 50/50 with me. Remember nobody is to know about none of this under any circumstance."

"I got you, no problem on my part." Pablo says as Bianca pulls up in front of Alejandra's apartment. "Later, Shawtie."

"Mañana, Pablo." Bianca pulls off as Pablo walks into the apartment. It's 4 a.m. and he is high as a Georgia Pine and needs sleep. He pulls off his clothes and climbs in the bed next to Alejandra pulling her close. She opens her eyes, "Que hora es?"

Her breath kicking, "4 in the morning. Go back to sleep." Pablo places a soft kiss on her lips.

CHAPTER FIVE

"What's up with you player?" Pablo daps Ryan up.

"You know me, same old same old. Ducking and dodging. I brought you a pound of Urkel and some pineapple kush for you to try out." Ryan passes Pablo a gray duffle bag.

They're on a dirt road out in the middle of Collatsville so it's no onlookers or nobody in their business. Pablo is leaning on his Celica after he puts the duffle bag in the passenger seat. Ryan is leaning on his Chevelle SS, if a car was to travel down the dirt road one of them would have to move their car for it to get by.

"How much is that gonna run me? Don't hit my pocket too heavy dawg." Pablo states laughing.

"Shit, for you homie, 3 bands. That smoke is on 1000, ain't nothing around touching that. MBG if it is homie." Ryan says.

Pablo thought to himself about that Orange Octopus Bianca had last night. That shit was no joke, if this is better than that he'd go up the mountain to snatch it himself. Now onto the moment of truth. "3 bands, huh? Let me ask you something, I'm your homie, right?" Pablo's hand inches closer to his waist where his Glock residing for the moment.

Ryan looks bewildered by the question, "Pablo what you on? You know you my homie. I would ride to the gates of hell with you. Why are you coming at me like that?"

This a dumb muthafucka, "You know why and quit tryna to play me stupid! I ain't ya homie!" Pablo pulls out his Glock and shoots both of Ryan's knees out.

"Ahh! Ahh! What the fuck! Why did you shoot me? Take the weed dawg! Just don't kill me!" Ryan is on the ground with his hands up like that does him some good.

Pablo starts pistol-whipping Ryan with the butt of the Glock, causing blood to pour from his head and face like rain out the sky. "Fuck them drugs! You a snitch!"

"I…ain't…what are you…talking about! I…never ratted on nobody! I swear…on everything I love!" Ryan spitting blood and teeth out.

"Oh yeah, well then explain this you snitch bitch!" Pablo turns his car and pulls out a manila envelope and puts his Glock on the roof because Ryan ain't no threat now beaten and shot.

"What is that? I never even saw the envelope before dawg."

"Shut the fuck up! This is your muthafucking government right here in my discovery! You are the one who put Detective Johnson on me and caused me to spend five years in jail! Why? Explain that to me because I didn't understand it!" Pablo shows exactly where his name and statement were located in the discovery.

Pablo plotted for five years on who, what, when, where, and how to take care of the couple names in his Discovery. Ryan just so happened to be the easiest to fish for and catch.

"I swear…I didn't want to…but I had to… they…was going to send me…to prison. Neisha would have…left me…I wouldn't be able…to see my kids. Man…I'm sorry! Please…forgive me. I…won't tell nobody…nothing about this… I'm-"

Pablo cuts him off, "So you beg now after you swore on everything, and that's the funny shit. I can't stand someone who lies, but has the nerve to swear on everything without thinking about the outcome! Once a snake is always a snake! You definitely have nothing to say about this."

Pablo throws the discovery back in the car and picks the glock up, tuning out Ryan's pleading. "You the one said you'd ride to the gates of hell with me. Say hello to the red one for me."

Boc! Boc! Boc! Boc!

Four times right in the face, Pablo searches Ryan's car and finds another pound of Urkel and $15,000. Neisha and her kids are innocent in all this so Pablo will put the money in her mailbox. He grabs a gas can and douses Ryan's car with the whole gallon and sets it a flame before driving off down the dirt road.

:Where you want to meet and what time: he texts Bianca.

The reply comes back in less than a minute.: Ham's at 2:

:Bet:

Next he hits up BB, the phone rings a few times before it is answered. "What's good?"

"Out in da field, ya already know. Where are you at?" Pablo asks.

"I'm at the Big Lots in Lenoir with Shawna. Where are you?"

"I'm headed that way, give me about 20 minutes and I'll meet you at Captain D's." Pablo can hear BB talking to Shawna in the background. Shawna is a known thot, but she about that paper. BB comes back on, that's cool my nigga. I'll drop Shawtie off and be there. Do you need anything special?"

"Nah and bring Shawna with you, it ain't nothing like that. See you in 20." Pablo ends the call then texts Alejandra.

:See you 2nite wear that shit I like:

The reply comes back :I got you Daddy:

Pablo pulls into the parking lot of Captain D's, he reloaded the Glock already so he uses a baby wipe to get the blood off the butt before replacing it on his waistline. He'll toss it off to the river later. He gets out checking his # 2's and Polo jeans for specks of blood. When he spots some on his J's he uses another baby wipe. He keeps both wipes in his hands and enters the restaurant after walking the 20 steps to get there.

When he enters he tosses the wipes into a trash bin and then proceeds over to the booth where BB and Shawna are sitting and chowing down. "Slide over Shawtie and let me rest my weary bones."

Shawna slides her 5' 3", 115 lb frame over so Pablo can sit down. "What's up boy? Ain't seen or heard from you in forever."

BB slides a tray over with two fish filets, a mound of hush puppies, and a bottle of water. "Thanks bra, and it ain't been forever, I just been busy since I've been home. I gotta get this paper up."

"What's good though? What up with the boy Ryan? He cop that?" BB asks, stuffing a hush puppy into his mouth.

"Everything is kosher. Shawna you still at the same spot?"

She finishes swallowing her food and then answers Pablo, "Nah I'm over at Edgewood. Why what's up?"

Pablo looks around and the only people in there are too far away to overhear. "I know you about dat paper and before I left, Meka and you was selling that fire, how come you stopped?"

"Well when Meka got wit DJ she flipped da script on a bitch, so I got a little job at Dollhouse and hit dem niggaz pockets."

"Shit ain't nobody trappin over at Edgewood nor Westview Street? It's a little paper on Kentwood, but then nigggaz pussy. Trap busted on them a while back and no return happened. BB throws out there.

They finish their food before another word is spoken, Pablo is the first to break the silence, "Shawna I got a whole pound of some Urkle, can you move it over there without smoke?"

"Shit I can move it at work just the same as I could at the crib." Shawna replies.

"Nah to the at work Shawtie, that's too much of a risk, too much happening up there. Never take unnecessary dangers or risks. What can you sprout back?" Pablo asks.

"Alright, I can feel that, I can do it a few different ways. We are going to want the most back. So –" BB interrupts Shawna.

"Damn straight. got to get us much-" Pablo stop BB.

"Let her finish talking first then you add your two cents."

BB hates being corrected by anybody, but he knows Pablo right so he motions for Shawna to continue.

"Like I was saying, I can bust it down to gram caps at $20 or quarters for $75 or sell a whole onion for $400. The caps a pop more, but it's up to you, how you want me to play it? My room-mate Cheryl can help." Shawna takes a sip of her drink.

Now BB starts spitting the numbers out like a calculator. "The caps produce $600 in an O, which at 32 O's would be $19,200. Take about three or four dollars off due to smoking and what-not. The quarters bring $700 an O, so that would be $22,400 more or less. We lose on the ounces, I go with both."

"I agree, Shawna I don't care if you smoke your share or not. Which I know you won't because you love that dead man too much."

"Damn skippy boy!" Shawna says laughing.

"You can get your roommate to help you, that's all on you. Just make sure that BB and I get six bands in our hands a piece. That leaves you 6 to split with your roomie. How long will it take you?"

"I can move it in no time once word gets out, so I say no more than a week. Is this a one-time thing or what?"

"That depends on you and how the spot does, I got it now so let's go." Pablo gets up and Shawna and BB follow him out.

CHAPTER SIX

P ablo walks into Hams at exactly 2 o'clock. He looks around and in the far right booth, he spots Bianca and walks over and takes a seat across from her. Pablo notices she doesn't wear any makeup, just a hint of lip gloss on her thick lips. She looks more tastier than anything on the menu.

"What's up Shawtie?"

"Nothing and we have to eat fast because we got a little job to do. So you ready?" Bianca asks, staring into Pablo's eyes. See's no fear just a look that has kill mode all over it.

"Alright with me, I came out of my mother's womb ready in case you didn't know. Let's order then shall we." Pablo calls the waitress over. "Let me get two lemon smoke flounders, an order of fries, A slice of cheesecake and a bottle of water."

"What about you Ma'am?" The waitress asked Bianca.

"Give me the filet mignon, baked potato, red velvet cake and a Diet Sprite."

"Will that be all?"

"Yeah, we're good." Pablo tells the waitress and when she walks off he asks, "What's the little job we got Chica?"

Bianca goes into her purse and pulls out a picture of an older white man. Then she hands Pablo a new paper clipping, "Read that."

He begins to read the article which says that Richard Hawkins, 52, of Boston, Massachusetts was charged with six counts of statutory rape. It was later dismissed for unknown reasons, but it is to be believed the family was paid off. Pablo hands the two items back to Bianca. "So statements were retracted, but how come the state still didn't push forward?"

"Both families are well-known and highly-regarded in Boston."

"So this is to be done when and how?" Pablo asks and before he can get an answer their food is delivered. They chow down and just make small talk while they eat.

After paying and leaving an enormous tip for the waitress they stand outside in the parking lot next to Bianca's Maserati. She looks radiant with her black hair curling down her back to stop above her ample bottom. She has some Gucci open toes with an all black Gucci dress, and purse to match.

"So what time are we leaving?" Pablo asks as he opens her car door.

"As soon as I get us to the airport. I will follow you to drop your car off and then we'll take mine to Charlotte for the flight to Boston. Everything is already waiting for us when we arrive." Bianca slides in the driver's seat.

"Well let's get to it then, no time like the present. Hope you can keep up. Later Chica!" Pablo closes her door before she can say or ask what he means.

Pablo jumps in his Celica and spins out as if he's at the Daytona 500. He is swerving in and out of traffic at reckless speeds, running through red lights, he takes the back way into Hilltop thinking he lost Bianca, but she is right on his bumper when he parks next to Alejandra's Focus.

He gets out and holds up his finger for Bianca to wait as he ducks into the apartment. He dashes upstairs and puts his glock in the locker safe of the closet. He then packs an overnight bag with his robbing gear. He stops in Alejandra's office and explains that he gotta go out for a couple days.

"Just be careful baby, know that I will miss you every second you're gone." He wraps her in his arms.

"Know it's the same and I'll make it up to you. I promise." He then proceeds to tonguing her down and squeezing her ass. He pulls back, "Te Amo Charpara."

"Te amo mucho Papi." Alejandra kisses him again and then he's out the front door.

He jumps into the passenger seat of Bianca's Maserati. "I'm ready Chica, let's roll. You got some of the orange still? I got some pineapple kush if not."

Bianca doesn't reply, she just pulls off and turns up "Gangsta" by Kat Dahlia. She turns left and then takes a right on 321 to get down to 85 and then head to Charlotte. Pablo pulls out the pre-rolled philly with the p.k. And lights it. He doesn't know what her problem is, but he knows he's gonna find out.

"So what your problem Chica? Ain't no way Imma ride 45 minutes with you over there sulking, nor on the plane to do the job with you sulking. So get it off your chest." Pablo passes her the blunt which she takes. They smoke two blunts before Bianca talks and when she does you can tell she is truly pissed off. "For one, I don't give a flying fuck how you drive! If you wanna kill yourself in a crash go ahead! Be my guest! But never ever do that again unless we're leaving a crime scene and have no choice! You can not be drawing attention to yourself and definitely not me!"

"Chica that shit ain't serious enough for you to have your panties in a wad. So furthermore don't tell me how to drive my whip! Plus, I know what I'm doing and my attention ain't your attention."

"See that's where you're dead wrong! When you're with me, anything you do draws attention to me! Same as whatever I do will draw attention to you. So, yes I can tell you how to drive when I'm with you or following you and it's vice versa. So respect it!"

"Listen, we're not gonna go back and forth about that dumb shit, its cool and you absolutely correct. My bad, I apologize and

I got you. The less attention the better off we are, I was just playing with you. You know cat and mouse. You handle the wheel well." Pablo lights the last p.k. Blunt he has rolled up.

"Apology accepted. You're still crazy and it's cool to play. Just be careful how you play and remember what I told you: I learned how to drive like that at the Nascar school." Bianca takes the blunt.

"Yeah, and I learned from Jimmie Johnson!"

"No, I'm dead serious, you can pay $500 for two laps without cars on the track. $800 with them, you should try it sometime."

"I just might one day. Anyways…"

They landed in Boston at 7 and rented a car from Hertz and got to the hotel on Center Street around 8. Bianca gets them a room with a king sized bed and tells Pablo, "Don't get no funny ideas. I'mma go freshen up then we'll go over and devise a plan of action."

Pablo lays down on the bed without even kicking his shoes off. He realizes he dozed off when he feels Bianca shaking him, "Get up sleepyhead and get cleaned up. I don't sleep with dirty people!"

"I got you, how many different beds do you sleep in?" Pablo says going into the bathroom. When he comes out 20 minutes later he sees McDonald's bags on the table in the corner.

"Here's two doubles, two chickens, fries, Mcflurry, and apple juice with a blunt of Orange Octopus on the side. Eat up as I fill you in and let me know what you think." Bianca says as Pablo pulls out the chair and sits down to devour the food.

"Thanks for the nap and food, Chica. Let me hear it and I'll add in where I feel the need to."

Bianca gets up and walks to the bed and squats down to pull a briefcase from under the bed. She comes back to the table placing the briefcase on top opening it, "Here's a glock nine, a 8" rambo knife, plastic ties, a pair of gloves, a ski mask, and lastly a fake ID."

"Where do you get all this on such short notice? I know I didn't sleep that long." Pablo asks.

"The ID I already had, the gun and knife I picked up when I was out. Anywhere we go it will be someone with whatever we need. I have my stuff too. So, here's the plan, Hawkin owns

Whole Foods at 413 Center Street, he drives a Cayman S all yellow. He leaves every morning at 9 to go to a D & D restaurant in Jamaica Plain. I'll drive and you make it look like a carjacking gone wrong." Bianca leans back in her chair.

Pablo finishes the food and lights the blunt. Halfway through the blunt he speaks, "Chica, I have no problem with your plan, only thing is I don't like the end. I gotta get a better idea and you are still only driving and it makes it safer. Imma carjack the fool and we're gonna go for a joyride before I end his life. Are you cool with that?"

"Yeah, as long as it doesn't cause unwanted attention to us."

"Nah it ain't, you just follow us out the parking lot and stay right behind the Porsche. Do not let no one get behind me under any circumstance. Do you know where some woods are?" Better yet a park?" Pablo asks, going to lie down on the bed fully clothed.

"Hyde Park. It's over on or off Lamartine Street I believe. Why?"

"You'll see, in the morning, good night Chica." Pablo kicks off his J's and goes to sleep.

"Wake up! Wake up!" Bianca pushes Pablo's shoulder until he is sitting up.

"Breakfast is on the table, go wash up. Everything you need is in the bathroom."

"What time is it?" Pablo asks getting up stretching.

"7:30." Bianca says, pushing him towards the bathroom.

Ten minutes later and he's eating as they head out the motel room. They get into the rented Toyota Camry and Bianca pulls out and heads south on Center Street to the Whole Foods parking lot.

"Thanks for breakfast, next time I get it. When you pull in the lot, drop me off right next to his car and leave for an hour." Pablo checks the Glock and places it in his waistband. He hooks the knife to his belt loop, slides the gloves on and lastly puts the skullcap on his head.

"What about the ski mask?"

"It goes on before showtime. When you pull in just go by his car on my side and keep going right through. In one hour come back, but park at the opposite end and when you see his car back out get directly behind it."

"Okay. Agarala. Just be careful and remember no unwanted attention." Bianca says pulling into the Whole Foods lot. "There's his car."

"Agarala Chica. Be back with you soon as I can." Pablo says this laughing. He pulls the ski mask over the skullcap and as soon as Bianca is by the Porche he rolls out and disappears. Bianca keeps wondering how the hell he do that.

Pablo rolled under the car and used the rambo knife to disengage the alarm. He then rolls from underneath the end and pops a small hole in the passenger window, he then takes the 5 inch piece of metal hanger Bianca didn't know about to pull the lock up. Easy as taking candy from a baby.

Richard Hawkins slides into the driver's seat of his Porsche and starts the car when he feels the glock on the back of his head. "Don't scream nor make any sound or you will die right here. Now back out and head toward Hyde Park."

"I'll give you anything-"

"Didn't I say don't make a sound? Now, drive bitch!"

When he pulls into Hyde Park, Pablo directs him to the back of the park, it's still a lot of people out. Fuck it go hard or go home.

"Let me ask you something and the more honest you are the better it is for you. Deal?"

Richard lets out in a weak voice, "Yes. Please mister. I can give you whatever you want. I have money, jewelry-"

"I just want answers, why do you like sleeping with underage girls? All these hoes out here and you want some girl that could be your daughter. Six times. Explain that shit to me Richard." Pablo slides into the passenger seat and see's Bianca parked next spot over.

"I don't know really, I guess because they make me feel young again. I never actually meant for it to happen, she wanted it just as much as I did. I swear I will give you whatever amount-" Pablo cuts him off with a slap to the face.

Smack!

"Shut the fuck up with that money bullshit! You a sick fuck!" Smack! Smack! Smack! Smack!

Richard's nose is bleeding and he's crying. "Please-"

"Shut the fuck up! Stay right where you are, don't move!" Pablo gets out of the car and walks briskly to the driver's side and opens the door to drag Richard out, "Let's go, Chomo!"

"Please-" Pablo smacks him again. This brings unwanted attention from passerbyers. Fuck it.

Pablo gets him on the sidewalk and trips while pistol whipping him into unconsciousness. He lifts up his shirt and pulls out the knife and engraved RAPIST CHOMO on his chest and drops the knife.

Boc! Boc! Boc! Boc! Boc! Boc!

"6 for 6 bitch!" Pablo hears sirens in the distance, he jogs over to the Porche and backs out with Bianca right behind him.

CHAPTER SEVEN

Here's your 6 bands and I gave BB his already. This is my girl Cheryl. Cheryl this Pablo. So when can you hit my hand again?" Shawna asks, all of 5'3", 115lbs and looks like Trina, just not as much ass. Her roommate Cheryl is 5'6" and around 140lbs, dark chocolate but she carries her weight well.

"Nice to meet you and I got another one in the whip. Listen, Imma hook you up with the Urkle, but Imma drop you some different strains over here tonight. It's some shit called Orange Octopus, I got to have 15 bands back. You keep the other 10 bands between yall. Only sell the gram caps for $30 and quarters at $200. I don't know what it actually comes to, just have me 15. Cool?" Ain't no way he letting it out he cooked Ryan's noodles.

"Yeah, Imma walk with you out. Thanks too and I won't forget the lookout."

"Don't sweat it, just stay up on your P's and Q's. One day I might need you for a lookout." Pablo tells Shawna.

Pablo gives her the gray duffel with the pound of Urkel and reminds her about tonight before peeling off in the 2006 Mazda RX8 Shinka that he dropped $8,000 for when he got the 30 bands from the Boston job. He put Black Cherry paint on it with a set of Lexani 22's, and tossed light cream inside. In Japanese, Shinka means evolution or transformation. Pablo tried to buy Alejandra a new whip, but she wouldn't hear of it. She said she loves her focus. Would he understand because she paid for it? So he just gave her 10 bands and splurged on his daughters. Next, go around and he'll hit his brothers up. He dropped his mom some bands, dropped Tameka some for Butterstreets. He has 4,000 left, but he got the flip and extra that's going to come in from Shawna and Cheryl.

He hits up BB, but still can't get no answer. So he texts Alejandra to meet him in front of the apartment in 15 minutes.

Bianca and him have been back a week and have only texted each other. Which is cool with him, he's ready for another job. As soon as he pulls onto Connelly Springs Road to give Alejandra a little more time he sees blue lights.

"Shit!"

He drops the nine he has in the hideaway under the dash that Sergio put in for him with the paint and upholstery job. He drops the ounce of Orange Octopus in there too. He hits Alexis on the phone.

Tap. Tap. Tap.

Pablo rolls down the window, "What can I be of help with today Detective Johnson? Wait, let Ms. Martinez know, she's on speaker."

"Detective Johnson, it seems to me that you're stalking my client. What is the meaning of this?" Alexis's voice comes through the speaker.

"Mr. Valdez is wanted for questioning in a homicide investigation. So you can meet us downtown at headquarters. Let's go, step out." D.T. Johnson backs up a step.

"How about a drive and you follow me downtown? How does that sound, Ms. Martinez?" Pablo asks, knowing the answer.

"Is my client under arrest?"

"No."

"Pull off and I'll see you downtown." Alexis hangs up.

"Well, you heard what my lawyer said. Adios." Pablo pulls off leaving D.T. Johnson looking like the cat who ate the canary.

Pablo sits in the interrogation room with Alexis on his left side. Their waiting on D.T. Johnson and any other party comers.

"Chica, on the real you look good enough to gobble right now. What's up Alexis? Have you ever got down in an interrogation room?" Pablo asks, smiling.

Alexis has on some Steve Madden pumps with an all-peach Fendi dress.

"Boy, right now is not the time and you know damn well I never got down in one of these rooms! You're a crazy ass and we've been there before." Alexis says reminding Pablo of their teenage years.

"Yeah, and you know I'd drag your sexy ass up in this room. Fuck these clowns watching! Pablo flicks both his middle fingers at the one way.

"Pablo, chill out!" Alexis is laughing her ass off at his antics on the inside.

The door opens and D.T. Johnson walks in by himself. This is a joke Pablo thinks to himself. D.T. Johnson sits across the table and tosses a folder in front of Pablo and Alexis. "Take a look at that. Tell me you know nothing of that or how it happened."

Alexis opens the folder and it's pictures of a burnt car with a burnt corpse leaning, well for better description melted into the car door. Alexis closes the folder. "Begin your questions and I'll advise my client when and when not to answer."

"Can I take this and copy it at Kinkos?" Pablo asks dead face. D.T. Johnson slams his hand on the table, "Mr. Valdez this isn't a joke! This is a capital murder offense! I will not tolerate any nonsense in my investigation. Now, where were you on Tuesday, May 9th?"

Pablo is staring at the detective with murder in his eyes. If looks like it could kill, today would be the day the detective would meet his maker. "I plead the fifth, pig."

"Okay. That's how you want to do this, I'll be back!" D.T. Johnson gets up and walks out of the room slamming the door.

Pablo opens the folder and flips through all the pictures. He slides one into his lap, "I'm going to keep this one. What do you think?"

Alexis picks the picture up off his lap, "For real, quit irking him, we got to find out what they have on you. Let me do the talking and if you want to say something tell me by looking at me."

"Alright. Agarala. Fool needs to take a chill pill." Pablo tells Alexis.

The detective walks back in and tosses the paper on the table, "That is the phone records of Ryan Day for Tuesday, May 9th. You called him at 9:22 a.m. from 828-292-6363. Ryan was found burned to death with four shots to the face. The coroner also found bullet entries in his left and right knees. To top it off, he was beaten before death and his baby mother surprisingly finds $15,000 in her mailbox. So, what happened?"

Alexis asks, "So all you have is that my client called the deceased? How long was the call? Do you have anyone putting them together?"

"Ms. Martinez the call lasted for 52 seconds, and it was the last that was answered by the deceased. Therefore, I only can assume that it was your client and the fact that Mr. Day is the reason your client went away for 5 years! That is evidence enough for me! I will go to a grand jury with this-"

Alexis interrupts, "You would get nowhere with the supposed evidence! You yourself assume that is not enough for an indictment on my client. Are we done here?"

"Will your client at least answer the phone call to the deceased?" Alexis looks over at Pablo, "You ready to go? Because obviously, the detective is wasting our time and the taxpayer's dollar when he should be looking elsewhere."

"Yeah, I'm done here, Ms. Martinez. Like I said before, I invoke my fifth amendment pig." Pablo stands as does Alexis.

"I will get you one way or the other Mr. Valdez! You will slip and I'll be there to break your fall!"

Alexis spins around, "That was a threat and violates my client's 5th, 6th, and 7th amendments! Your superiors will hear about this detective!"

Pablo pulls Alexis' arm, "Let's get up outta here, be careful detective, and don't get burnt." Pablo has no idea how prophetic his words are. They leave with detective ranting and raving. When they get outside Pablo helps Alexis in her car and bends down and plants one on her cheek.

"Thanks, Chica. I got you this week, when can we do lunch?" Pablo is also glad he tossed that 9 milli out when he returned. Alexis starts her Porsche 911 Targa and closes the door rolling down her window.

"It's cool, you know I got ya back. Just please stay outta trouble and do not give them any reason to gun you down. You know the blue team has it out for all Black and brown men in this country. We'll get together soon."

"Alright. I got you covered and thanks again, Chica. Text me later." Pablo jumps in his car and waits until Alexis is gone to leave. As he is pulling out, he receives a text from Bianca.

:Meet me at BO's in 15 mins.:

:Bet:

Pablo pulls into BO's parking lot and circles the arcade lot until he spots Bianca's Maserati. He parks next to it and jumps into her car, "¿ Como esta, Chica?"

"Nada. We have to meet El Diablo in 10 minutes, he'll be here. Before you ask, I have no clue to what it is about. So, what's up with you?", Bianca asks while lighting a blunt.

"Nothing. On that dead man chase as always, I just left downtown. That Detective Johnson be on me like crabs on nuts. It wasn't shit except a pony show. I'm gonna get his ass one of these days. What's that you puffing on?" The smell is different from the orange.

"This that Dubai Green, it's fire too! I gotta slow down smoking so much. How Shawna and Cheryl doing?" Bianca passes him the blunt.

"Shit moving sweet. I just gave her the other pound of Urkel and told her about the orange I'm gonna drop off tonight. Told her I gotta have 15 back on that. I can drop some of this too, you got it."

"I gave you the two orange so let her do that and then we'll talk about this, cool?" She takes the blunt back.

"Yeah. It's just side money for us to spend on whatever. Plus, I get to look out for my homegirl. You can't forget those who was there when you was down. Loyal people are a treasure to be found."

At that moment, two black Denali's pull in, one in the back of Bianca's Maserati. The other on her driver's side. "He'll get used to meeting us and come with just one guard. Even though he knows you, business is different." Pablo and Bianca get out and get in the Denali beside them only after the giant got out and gave the go ahead.

"? Como esta, Bianca?" El Diablo asks.

"Bein. Tu usted?" Bianca asked back.

"I'm cool. Thanks for asking. Before we get to business, I need to ask you something, Tio." Pablo says it that way, so he distinguishes personal from business.

"Go ahead."

"What's up with BB? I keep texting and calling but I'm not getting no answer. I'm concerned about him." Pablo states sincerely.

"It's nothing, he has a new phone and I sent him up north for a little while. He will be in touch with you soon. Now, on to current matters, how do you enjoy working with Bianca?" El Diablo asks lighting a Cuban and cracking his window.

"We have only done one job, but I enjoyed working with her and look forward to doing so in the future." Pablo answers.

"Bianca said the same about you, so that is good on both your parts. I have one small request, from here on out when we meet do not keep your weapons on you. I have trust in you both to do me no harm and it should be likewise." El Diablo isn't really given a choice.

"I'm cool with it as long as Bianca is cool with it. No offense." Pablo answers.

"I'm cool," Bianca says.

"Okay. There is an envelope in your car, Bianca, that is your next job. Enjoy." El Diablo is letting them know business is done.

Pablo gets out followed by Bianca, they get into her car to see what lies in the envelope. Bianca opens it and reads it, then passes everything over to Pablo so he can read it. After he's done he gives the envelope back to Bianca. He lights a blunt she has in the console out of the many she pre rolled.

"So what do you think about this one?" Pablo asks.

Bianca puts the envelope under her seat, "We really gotta be careful on this job. I have never had one person with the status he does. What are you thinking over there?"

"I'm wit it, fool gotta go just like anyone else that El Diablo hands us. Like you say, we just gotta be super careful and super cautious and we can not afford to slip one inch." Pablo passes her the blunt.

"Alright. I will pick you up tonight at your place. Be ready to go at 8." Bianca says.

"Why can't I pick you up, Chica?" Pablo throws out.

"Alright. Be at this address at 8, it's on Stonewall."

CHAPTER EIGHT

Shawtie I'll probably be back in three days maybe four. I don't want you worrying or stressing. Come here and help me out." Alejandra comes in from the bathroom. She butt naked and Shawtie look like she dropped from heaven.

"What a present for me Daddy? Imma miss him and you while you are gone." Alejandra climbs up on the bed and takes Pablo into her hand, slowly stroking his manhood.

"Yeah, it's all for you Mami. Show my manz how much you're gonna miss him." Pablo puts his hand on the back of her head as she pops the head into her warm mouth, twirling her tongue around before taking him halfway down her throat.

"Mmm...mmm" Alejandra plays with her clit as she moans around the shaft sliding in and out her mouth. She flips her ass around so that her kitty is right above Pablo's face and as she deep-throats his wood he spreads her fat pink lips of her camel toe...

"A key of coke a get a nigga kilt/and a banana clip get his whole house flipped/bringing danger to the life of his home

boy/you can send em on but let me know I don't run alone boy/
bout my money"

Pablo swerves up into Bianca's driveway on Stonewall and cuts
the engine to the RX8 and hops out. Bianca lives in a one-story
brick house with a rotunda porch, it has a swing and a couple of
potted plants. Pablo rings the doorbell twice before it opens.

"Come in, make yourself at home while I finish up." Bianca
has on a green Ralph Lauren dress, her hair is up in a towel and
she has her small pretty feet out. She walks down the hall as Pablo goes into the living room.

The room is spacious, with a tan leather sectional, matching
tan leather recliner on each end. An oak table with a couple of
coasters and an ashtray. It's an entertainment center on the far
wall, it's pictures of famous Latino stars from Queen Selena to
J.Lo. On the mantel above the fake fireplace is what he assumes
are pictures of Bianca's family.

As usual, he starts walking around taking in the whole house
and after looking in two rooms and a bathroom, Pablo goes into
the last room and sees a red-stained nightstand with a Tiffany
lamp. The bed is a queen with Fendi Sheets, comforter turned,
and about 20 pillows. Bianca is in the corner praying with nothing except the towel on her head and a purple matching set of
Victoria's Secret's bra and panties. She is praying to Santa Muerte
who is the 8th archangel, Pablo had no idea Bianca believed in
La Nina Bonita. She has a black candle which isn't for evil, it's
the votive candle for La Nina Bonita's protection and vengeance.
She also has a red votive candle which is normally used for love.
She has a green votive candle which is used for crime and justice,
some use yellow for this instead of monetary purposes.

The shrine that Bianca has of Santa Muerte is skeleton clad
with the jewels and robe holding a globe and scales. The globe
represents death's dominion over the Earth and is seen as the
tomb we all return to. The scales allude to equity, justice, impar-
tiality, as well as divine will. Pablo sheds down to his boxers and
lights a blunt kneeling down next to Bianca blowing a cloud of
smoke onto the shrine.

Pablo keeps his shrine in the closet of Alejandra's office to keep it out of sight, the reason being Alejandra is a devout Catholic. Pablo lays the blunt at Santa Muerte's feet, he calls her by the Senora de las Sombras (Lady of the Shadows). Pablo took up Santa Muerte (Holy Death) practice in prison from one of his cellies, Cholo.

Once Bianca finishes she gets up to leave Pablo kneeling where he is at and gets dressed, she has some questions for sure now. Pablo continues with his prayers for 15 minutes then blows out the candles and rises putting his clothes on, he leaves all the coins in his pockets on the shrine. He goes to the kitchen where Bianca hands him an apple juice and a ham sandwich. They eat in silence and Bianca tells him, "Let me grab my bag and we can go catch our flight."

"Alright. I'mma go to the car, yours or mine?" Pablo asks.

"We'll take yours this time, just please don't drive like you're at the Indy 500!" Laughing as she walks out of the kitchen.

Pablo lights a blunt walking to his car to wait on Bianca which doesn't take long and she literally floats to the car and slides in throwing her Fendi bag in the backseat. Pablo gets in and cranks up the car passing her a blunt while pulling out.

"I need to drop by Shawna's real quick." Pablo takes the right onto Harper Ave. He cuts down Trick Daddy's voice.

"Cool with me, our flight leaves at 9:30. Long as we make it by 9:10 will be alright." Bianca says toking on the blunt.

"We have one stop before Shawna's." Pablo says.

Pablo drops the two pounds of Orange Octopus off at Shawna's. He lets her know he will check with her when he gets back. As he speeds down HWY 321 Bianca asks, "So how long have you been a devotee of La Nina Bonita?"

Pablo switches lanes and turns up the volume a little on J. Cole's "Dollar and Dream III." I've been on the path for 4 years now, my homie Cholo put me onto her. I was always curious and asked questions about every belief that is in the world. I believe in God, the devil, angels, saints, so it's easy to believe in the Mother of Death. Life is death and vice versa, everything has to have balance. Santa Muerte is looked at as evil except to the small percentage that have the wisdom to know she isn't satanic. She is a fallen angel trying to win God's favor back and get out of purgatory."

"True indeed and that is the purpose that all humans are seeking. Have you thought about going to Mexico City to visit the shrine that Enriqueta Romero placed there?" Bianca asks lighting a blunt of Dubai Green.

"One day I plan on going and paying homage. Do you go to the Day of the Dead parades? I gotta hit one this year, probably go to Albuquerque or Santa Fe." Pablo pushes the needle to 105 and takes the blunt from Bianca.

"Boy if you don't slow this muthafucka down! You-" Pablo cuts up NF's "My Life" to drown her voice out. She tries to cut it down, but can't. Pablo locked the volume. The motor revs again as he switches back to 4th and redlines it into 5th.

He's swerving in and out the lanes on 321. He looks and sees the odometer needle touching 130, he starts dropping back down and unlocks the volume as he heads to Charlotte. He also notices her smiling.

They land in LAX at 2 in the morning, it's 5 am back in Carolina. They rent a 2015 Audi A3 that is pearl white over black. Bianca takes the 405 up to Santa Monica Blvd. and checks them into the Hilton on Wilshire. Their room is on the 20th floor and overlooks the city. They're sitting on the balcony the next morning smoking a blunt after washing up and eating breakfast.

"So how do you wanna do this or do you think my plan is good enough?" Bianca asks, blowing out smoke rings.

"I'm 100% with your plan, it seems like the easiest to pull off. I just know some fool is gonna try to buck, he's ex-military and sits on the board for the G-8 summits. Where are you going to pick up the stuff we are deciding on using?" Pablo takes the blunt from her inhaling deep drags.

"El Diablo has a person over on Ares Dr. It's in the suburbs I guess. Are there any other supplies that you think or feel we need?"

Bianca lights another blunt, her nerves are on a million and she can sense Pablo's radiating off the other side of the balcony.

He tosses the roach off the balcony, overlooking the city he says, "I'mma go down to the barrio, it's a homie I was on lock with that can handle some things for us. Don't ask just trust, I'll meet you back here in a couple hours. Cool?" Pablo stands up and looks down at Bianca with a look she knows too well.

"Cool. Just be careful because they are on some banging shit out here for real. Not that you are a duck, I'm just saying be careful."

"I know and aggarala Chica." Pablo leaves her on the balcony.

"Fuck!" Bianca lets out not knowing Pablo hears her as he is going out the hotel door.

Pablo took an Uber down to Lattimore St. This barrio belongs to a mix of Crips, Bloods, and Sureno. He's dressed in black forces, black polo, a white tee, and a white fitted to top it off. He passes by a group of youngins with red on so he knows he is in the right part of the barrio.

"Yo, lil homie you know where OG Red Balla? I got a dead man for you, if you go let him know Pablo Streetz is barking for him?" Pablo tells this to the one that is the ringleader of the group he assumes.

They surround him, all 8 of them and tryna to peep any fear. "Who you?" Yeah he chose the correct one.

He pulls out a knot and gives it to him, "There the dead man, like I stated, tell OG Red Balla Pablo Streetz. You handle that and I stay right here and give the rest of your squad comfort." Pablo leans up against a dark cherry Impala that has seen better days.

"Alright homies, hold it down and keep ya eyes open and alert." The ringleader takes off through the yard and disappears.

It's quiet and Pablo can tell that they are ready to earn a stripe, but it won't be off him. Where he has been and what he's been in, these gits don't stand a chance, not unless they are all strapped which he doubts.

"Yo homie!" Pablo sees the little ring leader, "Come on!"

Pablo goes through the yard and follows the little blood over one street to a one story house with a Grabbler Green over Black

Challenger sitting with some diablo rims. On the porch are about 15 red clad homies surrounding OG Red Balla. He jumps off the porch and gives Pablo a homie embrace.

"What's good my nigga? What brings you out to the West Coast?" OG Red Balla stands 6'1", 190lbs solid muscle with cornrows.

Pablo and him were behind the wall together, even though it was state time shit was crazy and they were thick as thieves. Pablo corrected one of his homies when he attempted to get some other homies of Carolina Cartel to rob OG Red Balla.

"Shit, dead man. I see you doing your thang as you said. Can we build for a minute in private?"

"Yeah. Come on to the ride. Y'all homies stay alert and don't let nobody bother us." He hit the locks and they slid into the Challenger. Red Balla lights a blunt and cranks the car so the 'LAX Files' by the Game spits out the speakers.

Pablo runs down the situation to him, leaving out Bianca and definitely El Diablo. When he finishes OG Red Balla says, "Dawg I can touch all of that, but something ain't adding up to why you want that shit my nigga. You need a hand. I got half the city wit me."

"Yo, on the real I can handle it and you know if I needed an army I'd ask you. Trust. I told you what I could and you'll see it on the news or in the paper. What is this gonna run my pockets?" Pablo asks as he takes the blunt.

"For you, 10 bands and don't be a stranger. We people and that is beyond this other shit. Can you sit for a few?"

"For you? Does a mite grow on a chicken's ass?" Pablo smirks.

When Pablo gets back to the hotel room he sees Bianca on the balcony sleeping. He looks at her and thinks to himself, one day. He freshens up after placing the duffel bag on the floor under the bed. When he comes out he goes to grab some food and sets it on the table before walking on the balcony waking up Bianca by blowing smoke in her face and falls back laughing as she starts choking.

"Chinga estupido baboso!" She jumps up and swings at Pablo who moves out the way easily. After she finishes coughing she goes to the bathroom. When she comes out Pablo tells her, "Mi malo Chica. I won't do it again, but you shoulda seen your face! Forgive me?"

"Fuck you, Pablo." Bianca states as she sits down to the table seeing the food. "Maybe, if this food is good."

Pablo went down to the family owned Mexican restaurant down the Ave and got El Tipico Montanero, chuzo de pollo, and ensalada frutas. After they eat and Pablo throws the trash away, he pulls out the duffel bag from under the bed. "Come here, Chica. Got some toys to show your sexy ass."

Once he gets the bag on the bed and opens it, he pulls out a Glock 9 for him, an HK .45 for Bianca, extra clips for both. "These vests stop any bullet from any weapon. These are stun grenades, gas bombs, and tranquilizers full enough to put a grizzly to sleep. Lastly, this." Bianca looks at the rocket launcher, "Where do you plan on using that? Are you tryna to take out a whole block or building? Where did you get all this? Do I even wanna know?" She sits at the table lighting a blunt.

Pablo walks over and sits across from her, lighting his own blunt. He puffs half of it before he speaks. "Chica. Sometime you're gonna wake up and realize that El Diablo ain't the only one who can reach outside their city. The homie I got that from doesn't know anything about anything. He and I go back a long way. Why are you in your feelings?"

"I'm not, and I never once said that El Diablo is the only one with connections, I have them too and not because of him. I thought we were doing this job as quietly as possible and you got a rocket launcher!"

"Chica that shit right there is the grand finale and I guarantee it's gonna make you orgasm! Wanna bet?" Pablo blows smoke towards her and Bianca blows smoke right back.

"What do you wanna bet?" Bianca knows this is a bet Pablo can't win. She has shot damn near every weapon and has never creamed on herself from doing so.

"One night in paradise with Ms. Bianca Gonzalez. What would you want if you somehow magically won?" Pablo asks.

"For you to kill someone." Bianca puts her blunt roach in the ashtray.

"That's it, shit I'd kill for you just on the strength of love I got for you. It's gotta be something else you wanna bet on." Pablo says before taking a drink of his apple juice.

"Understood. Just a yes or no and know the person I'm talking of could have everyone you love murdered."

"I don't care if it's the president, it's a bet." Pablo shakes Bianca's hand.

CHAPTER NINE

Pull up right there on the corner of Grove and Birch St. That's his stretch Lincoln Continental right there in front of the church." Pablo tells Bianca.

Church of Mormon. "Yeah, you see two bodyguards posted on the sidewalk and the one in the middle of the steps?" Bianca asks.

"Yeah, and you can't see him, but it's one behind the colonial pillar on your left at the top of the steps. Listen, when he makes his way out, wait until he is almost to the bottom of the church steps."

"That's four bodyguards that we can see, he has the other two with him on the inside. So how are we gonna stop 6 without drawing any gunfire to our thinking caps?" Bianca is nervous, but she ain't the only one, she hopes.

Pablo hands her the gizmo with three tranqs inside ready to go. He hands her two gas grenades and two stun grenades. "When you see me make my move, use that shit as you see fit. Just please don't accidently hit me with a tranq. We got this, 5 minutes to showtime."

"Can I ask you a question?" Bianca asks.

"I get to choose if I wanna answer it or not. I also get to ask you one back. Deal?"

"Deal. Why did you allow me to meet your family before we left to do this job?" Bianca is staring over at Pablo waiting for his answer.

Pablo stopped at his Mom's house where his daughters, nephews, and brothers were before going to Shawna's. He actually doesn't know why he did it. "To be 100% honest with you Chica, I don't have the slightest idea or reason why. Now, my turn, where's your family?"

"My mom was murdered, my father I don't know. I have a sister that lives in Aspen and a brother in Albuquerque. I-"

"Hold that train of thought Chica because here comes Thomas Trump now. I'm out, be safe." Pablo gets out and starts walking toward the church. He dressed up today in a Prada sweater vest, Prada dress shirt, Prada slacks, and some Del Toro loafers. He wants to look non-threatening and he slows his walk to give General Thomas Trump time to reach the bottom step of the church. Look like you fit.

When Pablo gets to the front of the Lincoln he pulls out his left hand from his pocket and pulls the pin and rolls the stun grenade like a bowling ball. He ducks, rolls backwards, and covers his ears.

Kaboom! Kaboom! Kaboom!

Pablo's ears are ringing and he turns to see Bianca drop two of the guards. The 2 that were closest to Pablo are down, the 2 that were following behind the General on the steps are pulling an unconscious General back up the steps. Not today buddy Pablo thinks.

Pablo pulls his nine and pops the top to the one closest to him as he sees the other one fall with a tranq in his neck. Bianca then lets off the two smoke grenades as Pablo runs up and fireman carries the General to the waiting Audi and drops him in the trunk before jumping in the passenger seat and Bianca speeding off.

They both start removing the plastic face pieces that El Diablo had made to change their facial appearances. "You alright,

Chica?" Bianca is sweating like a pig over a spit at a Southern barbeque. She wipes her forehead, "Yeah. I'm fine, what about you? You really enjoy this type of shit don't you?"

"Yep. It's the adrenaline high and knowing we are in control. You looked like a Xena princess warrior back there!" Pablo lights up a blunt.

"I was scared shitless! Why'd you shoot the one guard?"

"Chica, he had the drop and was gonna blast you. I couldn't allow that. No way, no how."

"Thank you. I owe you one, so you ready to finish this and get the hell up outta here? Because they're gonna tear this city apart looking for him." Bianca asks, taking the blunt.

"Yeah. Head on the Generals last stop so I can touch my feet on the Carolina Soil."

Bianca pulled into the hotel garage and Pablo snuck up on the worker in the security booth and tranq him good. Then he removed the video feed and placed a microchip into the computer's tower to erase the last 72 hours. After that he opened the trunk and tranqed the General and used the garage elevator to get him to the roof.

Bianca is standing off to the side with Pablo smoking a blunt and sharing a bottle of Patron. They are waiting for the General to awake, it's been an hour they have been up on the roof. The General awakened, it's been an hour they have been up on the roof. The General's hands are doubled with plastic ties, his feet are shackled and he's tied to a chair that Pablo pulled out of an alley by the liquor store.

"So what are you thinking about in that pretty little head of yours?" Pablo asks Bianca as he takes another shallow of the Patron.

"That he needs to wake up soon so we can get up outta LA. Speaking of the devil, he's coming around." Bianca walks over to the General and slaps him until he is fully awake.

When the General realizes his situation he starts in, "Do you have any idea who I am! I am General Thomas Trump! I'm a highly ranked official and you both can do yourselves the favor of letting me go unharmed! Or how would you like a long prison sentence in federal custody!"

Bianca pulls out her .45 and blows the General's left knee out. "You're the one who should feel lucky! We're doing the favor of not letting you go to prison to be butt fucked!"

Pablo has never witnessed Bianca this way before, maybe he should get her to drink more on a job. Pablo puts a gold and green bandana in the General's mouth, even though no one could possibly hear his screams of agony. Pablo reaches down into the duffel bag and pulls an envelope of pictures. He tosses them on the General.

"Your a sick perverted fuck and a waste of humanity! You're a waste of air! You're lucky you didn't go to prison because your ass would be named Amtrak. I guess your own people got tired of cleaning your shit up." Pablo kicks the chair over, thinking what a disgrace to the uniform he's wearing.

The pictures are of the General with underaged children of various ages and races. "I got something special for this sicko!" Bianca breaks a leg off the chair and pulls down the General's pants. She then rams the broken leg up the General's anus. He passes out.

"Chica you wilding! Let's turn da fuck up then! Get the rocket launcher!" Pablo then grabs the General and uprights him on the edge of the roof.

"What are you gonna do with the rocket launcher Pablo? Hold up one second."

Bianca walks over and produces a butterfly knife from off her thigh and in one swift motion drops the General's pinky dick and throws it on top of the pictures. "Now what?"

Blood is spurting everywhere, "Chica, I'mma sit him up and before he falls, pop ya cherry on that rocket launcher."

Pablo uprights the General and "swoosh" out comes the rocket and almost takes Pablo's arm with it and the General as the rocket busts through, spearing the General halfway down and exploding into the roof next door. Fuck it! What's done is done.

Pablo thinks as he grabs the duffel and Bianca drops the empty rocket launcher into the bag. "Let's casper, Chica!"

They haul ass to their room and get out their clothes taking turns to wash down in the tub filled with bleach. Pablo takes the duffel with clothes and the empty launcher to the incinerator in the basement. When he gets back upstairs police are everywhere and on every floor.

Bianca has food already laid out when he walks back in the room. "Thanks, Chica. So how do you feel?"

"I'm good. I actually enjoyed killing that muthafucka! I can't stand any man who takes advantage of any woman or child! I-"

Bianca breaks down sobbing, Pablo never saw her act like this, but he knows she has to get it out. He lifts her out the chair and sits on one of their lounge chairs on the balcony holding her on his lap. He doesn't say any words, he just holds Bianca tight with arms of comfort, understanding, loyalty, and love that is as sincere as the Earth's wind.

Bianca looks up after about 10 minutes of crying, tear streaks all down her beautiful face. "Thank you. I needed that, let me go get cleaned up. Then we'll eat and sleep before we get outta here tomorrow."

Pablo sits on the balcony thinking about a lot of issues that are tugging at him. It's like he's being tugged in two different directions, he's never been in this type of situation before. He pulls out his phone and texts Alejandra.

:You miss me Mami?:

A text comes back instantly. :Of course Papi! Te amo mucho toda corazón!:

Pablo texts back :Mismo! C U tomorrow:

Pablo then sees a missed text, it's from BB with his new number. He tries to get a hold of him to no avail. So, he texts him.

Bianca comes out freshened up and tells Pablo, "Lets eat." As they are eating there's a knock on the door. It's LAPD. Blah Blah. Thank you. They finish eating and lay down on the king sized bed. With the movie Love & Basketball playing. "You wanna talk about it, Chica?"

"Nah. I'm okay now, maybe one day, but not today." Bianca rolls over to face Pablo. Pablo turns to face her.

"Chica, listen, I remember you told me you killed one time before. I know it's different when it's personal. Know that I'm your nigga and if anytime you need me to hold you for any reason, I'm here. If nightmares come I'm only a call away. Any tears, no matter what I'm here." Pablo leans up and places a peck on her forehead.

When he leans back Bianca tells him, "Thank you and I know you mean what you say. I greatly appreciate it and if I ever need you I will call Superman!"

They laugh together and it feels good considering all the mayhem that is going on around them. "So who do you want me to murk?"

"Nobody. You won the bet, I creamed all down my thighs. A bet is a bet and I don't renig." Bianca says.

"Nah Chica, a gentleman never takes a woman on a bet. Go to sleep."

Pablo rolls over to dreamland, nightmares arrive from the past.

CHAPTER TEN

After Bianca and Pablo got back they met with El Diablo, gun-free, he actually gave them an extra $30,000 from the hit on the General. Pablo collected the $21,000 from Shawna and Bianca gave her two more pounds of Orange Octopus and told her next time she'd give her a pound of Dubai Green.

Pablo got his Mom a better house, hit his siblings off and got three acres with a 10 ft tall wooden fence surrounding the land. It's four bedrooms, three baths, kitchen, living room, dining room, and the front yard and back is big as shit. His bank account is sitting all right, they've done four other jobs for El Diablo and one was a double up so all but 20 bands went to the safe in his walk-in closet.

Pablo text Alejandra: you ready yet:

The text comes back: whenever you are daddy:

Pablo leaves to pick her up from her job, well she works for herself selling stocks and bonds. It takes him all of 10 minutes to pick her up and when she gets in the 650i that's mystic white over red designo, she turns down Jay Z's "Renegade" and plants a tongue kiss on Pablo.

"¿Como Papi? How was your day so far?" Alejandra buckles her seatbelt.

"I'm cooling, how about you Ms. Boss Independent?" Pablo takes a left on Wright St.

"I'm tired and need some good dick! But first stop at Mc D's. Your woman gotta eat to get her energy up." Alejandra rests her hand on Pablo's thigh.

Pablo takes a left on College then takes the right into the Mc D's parking lot. "You wanna go in or through the drive thru?"

"Drive thru. Order me the usual."

Pablo pulls into the drive thru and when he gets to the speaker he tells the drive thru clerk, "Let me get two McChickens, two Double Cheeseburgers, two McFries-"

Braat! Braat! Braat!

Boc! Boc! Boc! Boc! Boc!

Boom! Boom! Boom!

Rattaat! Rattaat!

Pablo feels blood splash his face as he attempts to react. Soon as he feels the comfort of the pistol grip in his palm, he lands into the black void of nothingness. He also knows Alejandra's brain matter is all over the side of his face. "This song is dedicated to my homies in dat Gangsta Lean. Why'd you have to go." DRS in heaven, I might just enjoy this afterlife after all. Pablo actually can see himself and he's walking on clouds that are sending comfort through his whole body with each step. All he sees everywhere are beautiful people with wings. Their bodies are perfect works of art. He's looking around for somebody he knows when he feels a soft tap on his shoulder. When he turns around he is greeted by the most exotic piece of dark chocolate he has ever witnessed.

"This way."

Pablo follows her and is lusting after her, her ass is twice the size of Nicki Minaj. She opens a door that is a cloud and he steps inside and the cloud room is a perfect thunderstorm except you don't feel the water or hear the thunder. Only can see it. His homeboy Wolf is sitting on a cloud that resembles a bud leaf.

"What's up dawg? Got damn we miss you! I know they got some good smo-" Wolf embraces him and steps back.

"I see you got my name inked. To business, cha non gon be here ta long. Ta know me look after cha and da family since me ben gon ta here. Cha needs to watch ya surroundings for dey enemies. The snakes."

"What does that pose mean? My circle is small as always and I know it ain't no slippery ones in my yard. I keep the grass cut low, who? Plus, if I'm here that shit doesn't mean nothing anymore anyways." Pablo sits down on a cloud chair and instantly feels a peace like no other.

"You are in the inbetween, which dey call purgatory. I was the one who got chosen to come talk to ya and let it be known, Alejandra is dead, she's up in the super heaven. She says be happy and quit while you're ahead."

Pablo jumps up, "What da fuck you mean Chica dead? Dawg you speaking crazy right now and if it's true, then any muthafucka hand involved is going to look at the top of a church! Chill and quit over my corpse! That's the only way I'm gonna chill or stop my mission."

"Cha wan sit down now! God make no mistake! Der is only one no matter the name someone attaches to. I, me, went before thee and asked your life not be done. Cha doing good deeds, but it's not for you to judge no man."

"Dawg no offense, I belong to Senora las Sombras, the lady of the shadows. Mi corazon is la Dama Poderosa, the powerful lady. I ain't ready to leave Earth, yet if today the day don't stand in my path! If it ain't then I'm gonna do what needs to be and should be done!"

"Listen to me, it is not your day because God chose it not to be and I plead before thee for you! Next time it's over! It's things in play that you know nothing about and for that matter will never know. I am telling you that you have to be careful every step from here on out. There is a snake in your presence, close to you and all you have to do is look, listen, pray, and it will be revealed. Plus we all know so we have to allow your free will to run its course. Stephen said let it go." Wolf stands and embraces Pablo.

"Whatever. One question, no two?"

"Yes everyone is here except those few who chose the in between. I already know the next question and I will answer it. Yes, 2PAC and Biggie are best of friends." Wolf walks through the cloud door.

"Thank you." Pablo hears Bianca's voice along with a lot of machinery, breathing tubes, and the beep-beep-beep-beep.

Pablo tries to open his eyes, they won't work, he tries to move his hand, his arms, his legs. No! No! I can't be paralyzed, I won't live like a vegetable. He tries again, beep-beep-beep-beep-it sounds faster and faster.

"Oh shit! Pablo hold on baby!" Bianca is yelling, "Help! Help! Doctor!"

"Ma'am what is it?" A man's voice asks.

"Please! Help him, I don't know what is going on!" Bianca is crying and Pablo is trying to open his eyes.

"Stand back! Nurse gave me 20 ccs of Nitrogen, 10 ccs of Ambit! He's tryna to get out of his coma! Hurry nurse!"

Pablo feels a needle in his arm, why the fuck they didn't shoot it in the I.V. drip. Ahh shit it burns, Doc what the fuck!

"Thank you doctor and soon as he wakes up I will let you know." Bianca says to the doctor. She sits back down next to Pablo's bed. "Pablo please wake up. We all need you, I know you're trying. Sinceridad fuerte!" Bianca is crying and Pablo knows, knows deep in his soul.

"La Dama Poderosa yo estoy Santísima Muerte rogar. Gimme strength to contra todas enemigos, that stand in my way. Light me protection against all law enforcement. Grant me justice for the wrongs against me, against Alejandra, my whole family. Protect me when I serve violent death upon my enemies and all against me. Give me breath!"

Pablo prays this and slowly opens his eyes to see Bianca head down. "Chica, hold ya head up." Pablo says and his voice is raspy. He needs water to coat his dry throat from not using it in months.

"Oh gracias la Flaca! Pablo is back!" Bianca jumps up and hits the button for the doctor. She jumps up and down like a schoolgirl.

"Water." Bianca puts a cup to his mouth and he takes small sips.

"Pablo I have so much to tell you, oh my God! I was so scared, oh my God, I'm so sorry! Alejandra is gone, they killed her! I-"

The doctor rushes in with a nurse right behind him. "Mr. Valdez, you're awake. This is excellent, you tried to come out a few times, but was unsuccessful. Now you did it and I will check you out and update you on your condition. Please can I have a moment with my patient."

Everyone leaves the room and the doctor checks everything, he takes the breathing tube out his nose and Pablo breathes with no problem. He has Pablo sit up slowly, moving his neck, arms, hands, fingers, legs, and lastly his toes.

"Everything is in working order, I'll have the nurse remove the catheter and down the morphine drip-"

"Doc, no pills, no drip, just regular I.V. cool?" Pablo says.

"Okay. If you change your-"

"I won't, when can I leave?"

"In about a week as long as your vitals remain the same. You're a very lucky man, especially to have family here everyday and that wife of yours to be bedside for the last 5 months. I'll check in again tomorrow, rest up."

The doctor leaves and Bianca is right back in the chair next to Pablo's bed. Pablo sees all the drawings, cards, balloons, and flowers around his hospital room and a lone tear drops out his eye. He hasn't shed a tear since he was a kid of about 10, this tear is for Alejandra, every family member, every homeboy, and most of all his soul. The next one shed will be blood tears.

Bianca wipes it away, "It's gonna be okay, I can not say I feel what you're feeling. I can not begin to know the pain, I just know it will get better and time heals all wounds. You just can never forget, everyone has been here everyday and they will be here soon because they know you're awake. We never left or gave up hope that you'd be back. I gotta-"

Pablo puts a finger to her lips, "Chica before everyone gets here I wanna say from the bottom of my heart, thank you. 5 months Chica, know I will never be able to repay you. I will never forget and tell me where Shawtie is buried."

"Weston Hill Cemetery. I made sure she had a proper burial, great paster, large tombstone. I videotaped it for you, I make sure the groundskeeper keeps it spotless and flowers are fresh every week. One shot is what did it, you were hit up bad. God, I feel so bad, I mean you laid up and I couldn't do-" Pablo quiets her.

"How many shots did I take?" Pablo asks.

"You like 50 Cent and 2PAC, only you don't rap about it, you like Master P, you bout it! Ten shots, most-"

"Daddy!"

"Daddy!"

CHAPTER ELEVEN

Pablo has been out of the hospital for two weeks and has been spending time with his family and that includes Bianca. She has been a God send, Pablo has basically been catered to on every level except sex. He has been working his whole body religiously 4-5 hours a day to get back right. He has bullet scars from the top of his shoulders to his feet. Lucky for him most of the bullets grazed, only three actually did damage. One took out a good chunk of his lung, one took out two ribs, the other broke his right leg. Those 5 months he healed up and the lung that was damaged healed back.

The doctors are stunned medically, but Pablo knows how it happened and everyday he looks up and throws a kiss and peace sign along with some smoke. They're gone but not forgotten as long as he has breath and walks the Earth.

El Diablo has even stopped by and said that he is going to get to the bottom of what happened. Pablo doesn't doubt him, he just remembers what Wolf told him and he's on point to the max. El Diablo told him when he was ready to let him know and gave him $100,000 as a get well gift along with a .50 cal gold plated H+K.

Pablo just finished working out and now he is at his shrine for Senora de los Sombras (Lady of the Shadows) Pablo has his in a green robe holding an hourglass (which represents death is not the end, but rather the beginning of something new) he uses this for the sign of patience. She also holds a lamp (symbolizes intelligence and spirit) which he uses for the light through the darkness of ignorance and doubt. Pablo has a blunt, some fruit, bottle of Patron, and candies underneath her feet.

He lights the white candle for gratitude, the red for lost love and new, the green candle for justice, and the black for protection in any and all unforseen battles. After he finishes he takes a shower and hits Bianca to come pick him up.

Bianca gets along with his daughters and all his family and he likes seeing her face light up with joy. Even though they don't have sexual relations they have love for one another. Their connection is deep and if that path comes they will travel down it together.

Pablo calls Alexis, "Hello. How is my favorite man in the world doing today?"

"I'm good, how am I your favorite man and you ain't throwing that pussy my way?" Pablo walks outside to wait on Bianca.

"Boy stop playing! Is that all you can think about? Wait, I know the answer, yes! You're crazy, how do you feel?" Alexis was at the hospital just as much as anyone else except Bianca.

"You've known me too long Alexis. On the real, thanks for everything. I know shit is hectic and we don't hang out like we should, I'mma try to do better. Bianca told me how you were crying in the hospital, you should know I wasn't going anywhere. Not until I get some more of you!" Pablo lights a blunt of Granddaddy Purple.

"Whatever and of course I was crying, I love you and even though plans don't go how we see em, you'll always be in my heart. Can you hit me later, I gotta go into court." Alexis sounds sad.

ANTHONY PAUL

"I got you and cheer up before I wax that ass up!" Pablo hangs up as Bianca pulls into the driveway in her Maserati.

Pablo jumps in and looks at Bianca in her Donna Karan dress and heels with her hair in a French bun and lipgloss shining on her thick lips. "Thanks Chica. Let's roll, I'm ready to get back to work."

Bianca backs out of Pablo's driveway and takes a left on HWY 64. She cuts down Jay-Z's and Beyonce's "On The Run Pt. 2" "Let me text El Diablo and see what's up. I left to go handle some business and didn't make it back in time to make your breakfast."

"It's cool Chica, I know how to cook and I'm healed up. Besides you have a life also, you helped me back, don't let it become a job. I appreciate every second Chica. Thanks." Pablo says lighting another blunt.

"I know, it's just that you're a big part of my life. We're not just partners in crime, you're my friend. Friend's stick together, remember Whodini?"

"Chica, that song is still pumping today. That's the real Hip Hop back then."

"Let me ask you a question?"

"You can, I'll decide if I wanna answer it and I get to ask you one back. Deal?" Pablo says.

"Deal. Why do you always call me Chica or Shawtie and never Bianca?" She takes the blunt from Pablo.

"Because you're dear to me and my movement. I think your name is beautiful just as the owner, and I will call you Bianca if you want." Pablo answers her.

"Nah. It's cool with me, no one has ever called me either of those until the night I met your crazy ass!" Bianca pulls on the blunt.

"Who'd you plant for worm food? Your choice to answer or not." Pablo takes the blunt from her and finishes it.

Bianca grips the steering wheel so tight her knuckles turn white. She takes a few minutes and then answers Pablo's question. "Julio. He was my first boyfriend, I loved him with all I had and he cheated on me. So I murdered him by my own hand."

Pablo decides to make the tension come down in the car, "Remind me to never piss you off Chica! So, What's up, did he hit you back?"

✦ 70 ✦

Bianca checks her phone and sees a text :twenty mins the old retail warehouse:

She shows it to Pablo and he tells her, "I'm ready to blaze something." He hits replay and fast forwards it to 3:30 on the Iphone that's plugged into the dash. "Deeper than words be on right/die for your love be on life/sweet as a Jesus piece be on ice/blind me baby wit your neon lights/" Bianca smiles.

Bianca pulls into the old retail warehouse parking lot, she pulls 30ft into where El Diablo has his Denali. When she parks the driver gets out and opens the door for El Diablo. He steps out in a Ferragamo suit with matching shoes.

Pablo and Bianca get out leaving their weapons in her car. When they get to where El Diablo is standing he leans in and kisses Bianca's check. "¿Como esta?"

Bianca answers, "Bein. ¿Tu?"

"I'm in good graces." He pulls back and shakes Pablo's hand. "¿Como esta?"

"I'm cool and thanks again for the gift. I'm ready to get back." Pablo tells him.

"That's good, listen Pablo, you're a good man and I appreciate the work you do. I have something else for you."

"And what might that be, no offense." Pablo has to keep his true feelings hidden.

"First things first, Bianca the envelope is in your front seat, it's very, very, important. The last time was hard, this is a little bit harder." El Diablo tells her.

"Okay, and we'll be more careful." Bianca says.

"Now, Pablo I left you an envelope also, but the contents are very disturbing and you do not handle them on my dime or time."

"No disrespect, but I don't ever intend to do either. Thank you." Pablo feels there is something not quite right, he just gotta see through the fog and the truth will jump out.

"None taken. Listen, I hate to cut and run, but I have an appointment." El Diablo gets in his Denali as the driver does.

After they leave, Bianca and Pablo get into her Maserati and they both grab the envelopes in their seats. "I wonder who it is?" Bianca tells Pablo.

Pablo opens his envelope and pulls out a stack of photos, he takes one look and puts them back. "Bianca drive to my house please."

"What are those pictures of Pablo?" Bianca has never seen his face so tense or have the murderous rage that she seeing and to top it off he called her by her name. "Okay."

Pablo thinks to himself, I can't wait to catch you niggas in public! I was loyal, I rode on every occasion and this is how it goes! He starts plotting his moves how Paulie taught him at a young age on the battlefield of the mental chessboard.

Before he knows it Bianca pulls into his driveway, before the car is stopped he's out. Bianca parks and follows him inside. "Pablo talk to me, please! Whatever it is, I got your back!"

Pablo tosses the envelope on the redwine coffee table and says, "Plies kept it too real." And plops down on the couch as Plie's voice comes through the speaker. He opens the philly box on the table and pulls out a pre rolled Dubai Green and lights it. "Bianca please grab me some that hard shit behind the bar."

Bianca does as he asks and hands it to him sitting down next to him.

"Pablo I don't-" Pablo waves his hand and holds his finger up in the one second gesture.

Pablo drinks half the bottle of moonshine and smokes four blunts before he says anything or moves. He gets up walking into the bathroom and opens the hidden compartment under the sink and pulls out a key. He places it in his pocket before flushing the toilet. When he gets back in the living room he tells Bianca, "Chica you looked at these pictures, what do you think?"

Bianca answers truthfully, "I don't know anyone in them, I recognize BB because I've seen him before. The other ones I saw in Hill Top, all I know is something going on that we don't know. Know this Pablo, I am with you 110%. There's no turning back until you get revenge on whoever you see fit. Just tell me how and when."

That's one thing Pablo loves about Bianca, she is down for whatever. She is a ride or die woman, she is always true to herself. Bianca is a bad bitch, one who you can brag about and she's even all across the board. "BB is El Diablo's son, his seed, so why did he let that be known? I can't figure that shit out right now. The other dudes are Carlos, Mario, and Joey. Joey fucks with Juanita, Carlos' sister. He is from the midwest, Carlos lives up in Bedrock half the time. Mario stays over in Catawba Ridge, Joey stays with Juanita in HillTop. Carlos got a bm that lives in Sawmills, Mario bm is over in Dulatown. Juanita works at Hickory Dickory Dock."

Pablo is pacing back and forth, he has a calm demeanor compared to knowing he was 20 minutes ago. "Well, if we know where all of them live then it's easy peasy. Who you wanna start with, we can turn them over to Santa Muerte esta noche. The job from El Diablo can be on the back burner for a couple days."

"Nah Chica, we're gonna go ahead and handle the Jefe situation first. Then when we get back we'll take out those three and I'mma handle that envy! Jealous! Trader muthafucka! Pussy ass bitch made disloyal faggot muthafucka! Sangre por Sangre! Corazon por corazon!"

Pablo rants for 10 minutes then tells Bianca that he is going to take a shower and pack his bag. She lets him know she'll be ready and go by her place later. Bianca has a lot of her stuff at Pablo's anyway.

CHAPTER TWELVE

Bianca and Pablo are riding in a rented 650i that's baby blue. Bianca is driving a 650i that's silver fox over falcon gray with bullet proof windows. The 650i their following has their next target along with his two bodyguards.

"You see that Benz with the strawberry paint that's two cars ahead of Harvey?" Pablo asks Bianca as he blows out a cloud of smoke into the Pennsylvania air, due to the window being cracked.

Bianca says, "Yeah, what about it?"

"That's the lead car, and I'm willing to bet that's his brother, attorney, and wife that are in that whip. Before you ask, I noticed that it slows down and the bitch throws fingers up signing before pulling back ahead. If we were closer, which is impossible, I could read that bullshit." Pablo tosses the blunt roach out the window.

"How do you know sign language? And if they are in that car, where are the other guards?" Bianca asks.

"I learned letter sign language in prison. The other car is either behind us or already at their destination. They're about 10 minutes out and we'll find out then."

"Well wherever they are we need to know how many exactly. So do you want me to turn behind them or what?"

"Nah Chica. Just drive on and I'll watch the rearview and we'll double back. This the wilderness out here, route 22 in the middle of a wrong turn movie." Pablo laughs at his joke.

"Alright. I hope it ain't no wrong turn muthafuckas out here!" Bianca laughs. "Let me ask you a question?"

"I get to choose an answer and I get one back. Deal?" Pablo asks. This is like a little game they've started with each other. "Deal. What is trust to you when it comes to a woman you are in a relationship with?" Pablo thinks for a minute and tells Bianca, "Trust ain't about her fucking another dude, its me letting her in on confidential information. My emotions, deepest thoughts, dreams, nightmares, my plans for my life. My fears, my tears, that soul wrenching shit."

Bianca slows down as the 650i in front does, the Benz turns right onto Chestnut Rd. The 650i does and Bianca keeps going as Pablo watches the rearview and no other cars turn off of Route 22. "They must be there already, so what now? Should we wait for the cover of darkness?"

"Yeah. Find a place to turn around Chica and we'll go back to the gas station to grab some food." Pablo tells her.

"You gonna ask your question?"

"What do you look for in a man that wants a relationship with you?" Bianca turns around using another side road.

"I look for a king, a man who deserves to be treated as a king. He gets that by treating me as a queen. By tuning into my emotions and detail to me. So that's how I know if it is the man I want. I want security and protection even though I can do that myself. A woman has to feel that with love and respect. Well, I do anyway."

"So, let me ask you this, do you believe in fate?" Pablo turns up Bruno Mars' "Just the Way You Are" just a little.

"Yeah, I do, I know that when we are born a path is already there waiting. We get old enough to start making choices, right from wrong, that is what changes the path. The obstacles in life change our paths, people we meet, and how our relationships are with them." Bianca says pulling into the gas station. "I'll go in and grab us something to eat."

"Alright. Grab me some candy too if you don't mind." Pablo says.

It's been two hours since they ate the gas station nacho's and Reese Pieces candy. Pablo finishes his apple juice and throws it in the bag from the store. They parked on a rutted path off Chestnut Rd. It's pitch black, crickets and frogs are making their night sounds. Bianca and Pablo are dressed in all black, guns locked and loaded.

"Chica you ready?" Pablo slides the nine on his waist. He snatches the bookbag out the backseat.

"Ready? Let's go and Pablo, be careful." Bianca touches his arm and their eyes lock with intensity for just a few seconds.

Pablo wants to kiss her, but he breaks eye contact sliding out the car into the black of night. "Señora de los Sombras, protect and guide me. Lead me through the shadows as only you are able."

They walk a ½ mile up in the woods and stop at the treeline. "It's gotta be sensors somewhere, motion lights, or a guard walking the grounds." Bianca tells Pablo.

"Wait and watch." They are looking at a minimansion holding Harvey Hillman, his wife Janice, James Franklin the attorney and Teether Hillman his brother.

They know its two bodyguards at least, it should be more. Hell the front of the house has a fence, I guess people don't think or plan for invasions coming from the side of their house Pablo thinks to himself.

"There goes one guard, wait there's another. See them?" Bianca whispers.

"Yeah. There's no lights popping on, they must be turned off." Pablo whispers back.

"They're gone, so that's two we know on the outside. Watch this and I hope it doesn't backfire." Bianca lays her .45 on the ground and removes a pack of half eaten Reese's from her pocket. She takes a few out and throws them in three different directions.

"What are you doing? Tryna attract ants." Pablo is joking, but really wants to know why Bianca is tossing candy into the yard.

"Yeah, but the ants that woulda been coming shoot. See if there were sensors where the candy landed, we woulda seen the guards. I'm thinking it's just the two guards outside, they're here alone."

"When the guards make their next round you creep one and I'll creep the other." Pablo tells Bianca.

"Okay. How are we gonna get into the house is the question." Bianca puts the .45 back in her waistband pulling out her butterfly knife.

"We'll cross that bridge when we reach it. Do you want the left or the right?"

"I'll take the left one and meet you once I'm done." Bianca answers.

They wait for about 5 minutes and they see the guards. Once they pass each other they wait one minute and move as one in the shadows of the night using the moon as light. Pablo creeps on the guard and puts him into a Charleston chokehold.

The guard's breath is automatically cut off, he tries to struggle but it's no use as Pablo lowers him to the ground. Pablo then stomps down on his neck twice breaking it. He keeps moving until he meets up with Bianca in front of the house.

"You straight Chica?"

"Yeah. How about you? You only knocked him out right?" Bianca asks.

"Nah. Don't worry about it, I can deal with any backlash. Listen, how do you wanna do this?" Pablo whispers in her ear.

"Let's just ring the doorbell. Whoever opens it we lay down, tie up, and get to our target." Bianca pulls out a taser.

"What about, fuck it, we know there's four people up in there. I'll take the top, you take the bottom." Pablo has the nine in his hand and tells her, "Get some ties out."

Bianca reaches into the bookbag and pulls out some ties, "What all do you have in there?" She zips it back closed.

"A few toys in case all hell breaks loose. Come on." They go up to the door, Bianca rings the bell and Pablo is to the left of her and outta sight.

After a minute the door opens and Bianca doesn't hesitate to use the taser. Pablo moves to catch the old man before he can hit the ground.

"This must be the lawyer." Pablo lays him on his side and they work as a team to gag and hogtie the man up.

Pablo silently creeps up the stairs, when he reaches the second floor he takes the right side. There's two doors, he opens the first one to see it empty, he enters and searches. Nothing. He goes back out in the hall and goes to the other door, it's a bathroom.

He turns around and goes the opposite way to the other side until he comes to the first door. He opens it to see a sleeping lump in the bed, he moves silently into the room. When he looks down he sees it's the brother, Teeter.

Pablo puts the nine on his waist so he can go into the bookbag extracting a small capsule. He grabs Teeter's throat causing his mouth to open and drops the cyanide capsule into his mouth. Teeter attempts to get up, but Pablo has already pulled his nine back out and places it to his head. "Don't resist. Just chew and when you awake you'll be fine." Pablo whispers but with the voice of a violent storm.

Teeter chews and starts convulsing as soon as he finishes the pill. Pablo holds him down until there is no more movement from his lifeless body. He searches the room finding a Louie suitcase with dvd's, jewelry, passports, about $60,000 in hundreds. As he goes back in the hallway he runs into Bianca.

"Shit!" They both lower their weapons and Pablo points at the suitcase.

"His brother, well now dearly departed. Did you run into anyone?" Pablo sits the suitcase up against the wall.

"No. Pablo, why did you kill him? This could lead to shit creek." Bianca says it, but her pretty face reads something else. A vampiress on the blood hunt.

"Come on Chica." Pablo goes to the next door and opens it, it's another bathroom.

They open two more doors and find nothing. The last door on the left holds the next victim of homicide. Harvey Hillman curled up with his wife, Janice.

Pablo rushes the bed and snatches the cover off the two sleepers. They both startle awake stark naked. "What the fuck! Oh no!" Harvey says, holding up his hands.

"Get out! Help! Help!" Pablo shoots Janice in her face.

Boc! Boc! Boc!

Bianca pops Harvey with shots to the head.

Boom! Boom! Boom!

They search the room finding two Louie suitcases with fake I.D. passports, for the deceased, some jewelry, each suitcase has at least $60,000 in hundreds. "There's gotta be more money. These muthafuckas were leaving the states and he's a multimillionaire."

"I'll go check downstairs, check anything we may have overlooked." Bianca takes one of the suitcases leaving the room.

Pablo starts going over the room again when he notices the bookcase shelf that has all the same books. He pulls down and it moves the whole bookshelf to reveal a safe. "Fuck!"

Pablo goes downstairs with the other two suitcases and sets them by the door. "Bianca!"

She comes from the back. "Yeah?"

"It's a safe, there's no way we are getting in unless that attorney knows the combo. Wake him up."

"Okay. I still say let's just go and take what we have." Bianca removes the green and yellow bandana they used as a gag. She slaps the attorney awake.

"Who are you people? If="

"Shut the fuck up or you will never speak again in this life." Pablo tells him.

"What's the combo to the safe in Harvey's room? Don't play games, you're the only one besides us breathing in the house." Bianca let's him know.

The attorney turns paler than what he is originally. "You killed Har-"

Pablo puts the nine to his head. "Combo or death. Last chance old man."

"It's 43215, and you have to use Harvey and Janices thumb-prints for it to open."

Boc! Boc! Boc!

"Pablo what the fuck! You didn't have to do that. Damn! Fuck it!" Bianca heads back upstairs.

"Pablo goes right behind her, "Chill out Chica. I got it worked out, trust me." They enter the room and Bianca walks over to the safe. "Gimme the blade Chica."

"Here, catch!" Bianca tosses him the butterfly knife. She watches as Pablo saws off the thumbs from both of Harvey and Janices hands.

"Let's do this and get outta here." Pablo wipes the blade, handing it back to Bianca. She enters the code and Pablo uses the thumbs, it was both the left thumb. The safe opens to stacks of hundreds. Pablo gets the pillowcases off the bed and they fill them up.

"This gotta be a couple million right here." Bianca says walk-ing out the room with Pablo following.

"Yeah, we came up, but we gotta spread it also. I'll explain on the way home."

They reach the bottom of the steps and Pablo gives Bianca the other pillowcase and tells her. "I'll be in the car in a minute."

He puts the money and jewels into one suitcase and opens the bookbag pulling out the toy he brought. He hits the green button and the times reads 3:00 minutes. It's a bomb with supposedly some kind of acid mix. He grabs the suitcase and goes to the car loading the trunk.

CHAPTER THIRTEEN

fter getting back to Carolina, Bianca and Pablo counted the money using a couple money counters. They came away with 3.7 million dollars in cash and $700,000 worth of jewelry. They used a confidential donation company to spread 2.4 million throughout schools in the Carolinas. To put food in churches and homeless shelters, salvation armies, goodwill and the cancer research center in Durham. They divided the other 2 million between them.

Bianca set up the offshore accounts and the one account in Switzerland. Pablo broke his people off and sent money to a few of his homeboys still on lock. He also sent OG Red BAlla 40 bands, he gave Alexis 100 thou, now there on the way to meet El Diablo at the old movie theater off Morganton Blvd. They're in Pablo's brand-new Donk, it's a 73 Chevy on Savini rims with 13" lips, 26X9 on the front and 26X10.5 in the back. The paint job is Carolina Tarheel Blue with a Tarheel painted on the hood.

Pablo learned all about the Donk game in the YAM, Swamp, MIA. He's dressed in all Ferragamo with a Bulova gold watch. He looks over at Bianca who is banging out the Bottega Veneta dress, the stellar open toe booties that show off her size 5 feet, with small perfect pedicure toes. The Eiffel Tower Drop earrings that are two half moon emeralds, at 6.60 cts that was a gift from Pablo along with the female version omega watch.

"You fly as shit over there Chica. Those emeralds look as if they were made only for you. Real talk." Pablo turns into the old movie theater parking lot.

"You ain't looking bad yourself, it's different from your normal dress code. So, we're gonna take care of the problem after we finish the meeting with El Diablo?" Bianca asks, referring to Carlos, Joey, and Mario.

"Yeah, it's definitely gonna be 200 on the level of TTG. I don't want you helping though. It's not your problem to handle or get mixed up in. Plus I could end up in jail and I refuse to let that happen to you. We lighting up the city after this meeting, that's why I'm dressed up." Pablo tells Bianca as they wait on El Diablo to arrive.

Bianca turns her body, placing her back against the passenger door. "Tu es loco, lo estoy haciendo." Bianca tells him she's doing it, meaning going with him to handle the problem.

"No, Chica. I can't ask that of you, nor will I, I need you out here if shit backfires on me. There are people I would need you to watch for me. Please respect my wishes." Pablo tells her hoping she will listen, but he seriously doubts that she will.

Before she can say anything else El Diablo's Denali pulls in and up to the Donk's grille. They get out and watch as the lone bodyguard gets out, then opens El Diablo's door. He steps out in an all white Armani suit with matching shoes. The bodyguard goes to pat them down, but El Diablo tells him, "No. Ello's bueno. ¿Como esta Pablo?" He asks, shaking hands.

"I'm straight. I wanna straighten the record about what went down in PA. That was all me, I know that it was one target and I killed six people with that explosion. Those DVDs are the reason I did it, Bianca tried to stop me, so it's not her fault." Pablo tells El Diablo and is watching everything with the precision of a hawk watching prey.

"Caminas conmigo, both of y'all." El Diablo says and starts walking in the empty lot. The bodyguard is a few feet behind them. "When I ask the both of you to do a trabajo, I expect it to be handled correctly. You are a team, one does not make a decision solo, by oneself. Es reprender, reprimand for your actions."

Pablo stops dead in his tracks, "Hold up, you ain't the one who is putting blood on their hands. We are, her and me! There is no risk for you, I already told you that I acted alone. On my own, and the job got done! Four people died that should have and I can't help the facts!" Pablo's eyes are on fire making him look demonic.

Bianca steps in front of Pablo, "I understand and I could have done more to stop Pablo, but I didn't want to. So, what is the reprimand so we all can move on from here. Business is business. Lo siento. I-"

Pablo moves her out the way, "Man fuck this bullshit! You don't like what happened then I'm done muthafucker! Oh yeah and ain't shit gonna happen to Chica, not while I'm breathing! Before I walk off let me ask you this, how da fuck I know the pictures ain't a setup? How da fuck I know your hand wasn't behind it? If so muthafucker you can pick a plot next to your bitch ass offspring!"

The bodyguard pulls out a .45 aiming it at Pablo. "No tienes que decirlo!" Just give me the word.

Bianca is trying to calm the situation down, she saw this look the other day when Pablo got those pictures. It's like a demon is trying to climb out his body. "Calmate! Please, let's not get carried away! This is what we cannot do, it will not solve anything. Pablo just let him explain and hear his side. Jefe tell macho back there to put his weapon down or he won't make it out of this parking lot."

El Diablo doesn't say anything, he has a smirk on his face. He finds all this amusing, he actually likes how Pablo reacted in PA and how he got the cajones to talk the way he is now. A killer always respects other killers, especially when they're so dangerous and Pablo is a bonafide killer.

Pablo turns all the way around and walks until his forehead touches the barrel of the .45. "Go ahead bitch! You a pussy if you don't do it! You-"

"Pablo, please! Don't insult or instigate the situation!" Bianca says.

"Man fuck this wanna be gangsta! I live this thug life! Chinga tu Madre!"

Bianca thinks this is it because that was one of the most disrespectful things you could say to a man. Fuck your mother.

El Diablo clears his throat, "Arriar la pistola." The bodyguard lowers his gun. "Pablo I'm an understanding man, as well as a great businessman, if I wanted you dead I would not have my son do it. I would let you see it coming, I have respect for you and truthfully I agree with what happened. Those above don't and want $50,000. Now it is your choice."

Pablo turns a little, "That's chump change, but if you agree then let it come out of your pocket. I appreciate the fact you say you'd let me see you coming, but I don't buy that." He means this like words that he prays daily.

"Pablo stop! I'll pay it, it's nothing-" Bianca is saying when El Diablo cuts her off.

"No. I will because those DVDs are a gold mine to the people above me. Now I will say this, Pablo I respect you have principles and are willing to stand for them and not bend. Like I said, I didn't try to have you killed so please do not ever threaten me again. Take my word as a man."

Pablo thinks and then replies, "I'll take your word as a man. We'll have to here in this deserted parking lot." Pablo turns in rapid speed landing a left hook followed by a right uppercut to the bodyguard laying him flat. "Tell your man next time he pulls a ratchet he best use it and he owes you his life."

Bianca and El Diablo watch as he goes to the Donk getting in and cranking it up. Lil Boosie "Hatin" blast throughout the lot. Bianca talks to El Diablo for a few minutes before coming to get in the car. Pablo doesn't say anything as he pulls off headed towards Shawna's.

Bianca doesn't like the silence only because she doesn't want Pablo in a foul mood. "These Eiffel Tower drops had to cost you a fortune, thank you. I have never had a man do anything extravagant before." Bianca lights a blunt, passing it over to Pablo.

As he takes the blunt filled with Dubai Green he tells her, "Money doesn't mean nothing to me. Money comes and it goes, you can have a billion dollars and not be happy. People that are around me deserve to be spoiled and happy. Your family got to be happy, I know how to really be happy, I know how to accomplish it at the bottom too. You're welcome and Chica if a man never bought you something it's because he couldn't afford it."

"Maybe that's true and I feel what you're talking about happiness. I remember times when I was truly happy, even though it was nine of us in a two bedroom trailer. Barely no food, didn't know where the next meal would be coming from. Where did you find these earrings though?" She asks, taking the blunt toking on it.

"Let's just say I got a friend who is Pakistani and he gave me the hook up. I got the girls some also, just 1 cts though."

"I know they'll love them. So what do you wanna do?" Bianca asks, passing the blunt back.

"I already told you, Chica and that's that. What did El Diablo have to say after I walked off? I know he was upset I knocked his flunky out. Fool better be happy I ain't send his bitch ass to La Flaca."

"He didn't say anything about that, he did restate that he didn't try to have you killed. Said he has the utmost respect for you as a man. He said that you and I need to get at James Tredwell, said he was shady, but not to what degree." Bianca let's him know.

"Talking about the politician that rents out spots for more than they are actually worth?"

"Yeah, one and the same. Do you know him or something?"

"Nah. I just know of him, I know who his daughter Jessica is though. I'll swing around to holler at her and scope out her dad. I don't believe that El Diablo ain't know what BB was up to, he knows too much as it is. I don't trust him period. What else does he have to say?" Pablo turns on Edgewood to go to Shawna's house.

"That he has an archenemy up in Jersey/Philly that he's been at ends with for over ten years. The guy's name is Archer and that BB is in cahoots with him to try some takeover shit together. That's his reason for giving BB up in those pictures."

Pablo pulls in Shawna's driveway behind the two Cayman all red Porsches.

"Chica, I don't feel like going in there right now. Could you go in, grab the 30 bands and take her the duffel out the trunk?"

"I got you, just smoke another blunt and I'll be in and out. Anything else?" Bianca gets out to get the bag out of the trunk.

"Let her know we need 40 back on that bag and let her know I'mma drop off 1,000 oxys later. They are the 60s so she has to get $1 milligram."

"Okay. I'll be back in a minute." Bianca walks up and knocks on Shawna's door. Soon as she steps in the house Pablo backs out and drives off.

Pablo shut his phone off so it will go straight to voicemail. Bianca was blowing it up with calls and texts, he knows she's pissed, but he told her what was up. He's outside Juanita's apartment in Hill Top, he didn't see her car so he just decided to chill until she drove up or he saw Joey in the car.

Hopefully he can kill all three of them together, if not he'll get them as he can. After three blunts he sees Juanita pull up, he waits until she is almost to her door before getting out his RX8.

"¿Como Juanita?" Pablo hollers at her. She turns around and sees it's Pablo. She knows him, but doesn't know him.

"Oh. Hey, how are you? Carlos told me what happened, I'm so sorry for your loss. What's up though?"

Pablo looks at all five foot two, 130 lb caramel skin and thinks what a waste of air. He knows she knows because she won't look directly at him. "Carlos and Joey told me to meet them here. I just pulled up when I saw you. They here?"

"Joey asleep with the flu, Carlos I don't know where he at, so who would you'd talk-"

"Bitch quit yakking and open the door before this nina puts your dumbass thoughts on apt 22." Pablo holds the nine against her face.

"Okay. Just please don't hurt me. I have nothing-"

"Shut the fuck up and get in the apartment." Pablo don't even give a fuck if someone's seen him or not. Once the door is closed. He walks her to the bedroom and sees Joey knocked out. He makes Juanita sit on the floor next to the bed.

Whack! whack! Whack!

Pablo wakes Joey savagely, beating him with the 9. He's muttering the whole time.

"Stop! Stop! I'll tell you everything! Please!" Joey is begging. Juanita is crying, but not making a sound. "BB came to us and said his-"

Whack! Whack!

"I tell you when to talk! So for now shut the fuck up! Juanita you need to open your mouth." Pablo tells her.

"Please don't hurt me, I'll do anything you want."

"I said open your mouth, cuz I'm about to put something in it." She does as he says, closing her eyes. He puts the gun in her mouth and pulls the trigger.

Boc! Boc!

Then he turns to Joey, "See you in hell."

Boc! Boc! Boc! Boc! Boc!

Chapter Fourteen

After Pablo dust crops his need to enjoy their brains all over the room he hightailed up out of there. He took his RX-8 home and called his paint man Sergio to let him know he needed new candy for the whip.

Now he's riding around trying to catch Mario or Carlos. He has rode by both their bm's cribs and ain't seen no sign of either. He's thinking about murking both their bm's, but they are innocent. He need to actually know, so if he finds out they did then ain't no maybe. His phone lights up with Bianca's number, fuck it.

"What's up Chica? I know you're pissed off and you deserve to be, but I'll make it up to you. I promise. Where are you at?"

"Meet me at Julia's please, come to the end of the road. It's a new house under construction." Bianca hangs up.

Pablo looks at his phone and hits her number back. Goes directly to voicemail. Before he can try to call again he gets a text.

:What's good my nigga?:

:Who dis?:

:BB:

This snake ass chump, play it cool, don't let fool in your game room. Pablo thinks to himself.

:What's up? How up top? When you coming back?:

:It's all good IBBS got to get this money:

:True. Listen I'm on a business venture right now so call me tomorrow:

:Alright:

Pablo throws his phone into the pocket of his cargo pants jumping in his GLC 08 and taking off to Julia's Place. He's wondering what the hell Bianca is doing out at an under-construction house. Plus it's over by James Tedwill, hope she's cool.

Pablo hits his lights on a GLC so he's not drawing any unwanted attention or to be seen until he wants to be. He's not worried that Chica is playing foul, it's someone else maybe trying to use her. If that's the situation then it's about to be some major fireworks even though it's not the 4th.

He sees the spot Bianca told him was there and also only sees her Maserati. He parks the GLC next to her car, soon as he is out the car he pulls out his nine. He pops the trunk, moves the speaker box to open the concealed compartment. He pulls out three grenades, an extra clip for the nine, and picks up the AR-15 with the 30 clip and two spares. He uses all the pockets on his cargo pants and the pocket on his black hoodie to carry his toys.

With the AR on auto and his nine tucked on his waist, he makes his way to the house. He creeps up the steps onto the unfinished porch. He doesn't hear nothing. He moves silently into the house and uses all the stealth mode that he can to seek and find Bianca first and foremost. Pablo gets to the back of the unfinished house to see Bianca sitting on the back porch steps. He steps outside, "Chica what's up? You okay?" Bianca turns ever-so-slightly and when she looks at Pablo she starts laughing. After she settled down she asked, "Why are you carrying an AR?"

"Chica I don't find shit funny! You hit me up saying meet you here, then I tried to call again, voice mail. And I'm coming here thinking of you in a situation and I'm coming to save your pretty ass!"

"Oh. Okay. Trust ain't no hostage situation on my part and if that ever occurred I'd let you know. Anyways, why the fuck you leave me at Shawna's like that?" Bianca stands up, she's dressed and looks the same as she did a few hours ago.

"I told you once and I'll tell you again. This isn't your problem, it's mine and I'ma take care of it. I already took care of Joey bitch ass. So if you will let me finish I can more than likely be done by the morning."

Pablo was staring at Bianca with a yearning she knows well.

"I heard you the first time and I'm hearing you now, but I think you need to understand me. You in a fight or war or struggle, down and out, up above all, I'm right there. That's what friends do, that's loyalty! Now I think you should go check the Porta-Potty that's right there."

Bianca points at it, it's a few feet from the back porch steps.

"Why the hell should I check a porta-potty?"

"Just trust me and do it, you'll like what you find." Bianca says.

"I don't remember telling you that I liked shit or piss!"

"Just check it, for little old me. Bianca throws in a little sweet voice. Pablo walks off to the Porta-Potty and opens the door. It takes him a minute to register in his brain what his eyes are seeing. Mario is beaten bloody, tied up and gagged up. "Chica, I honestly am at a loss for words. How did this happen? I thought that I explained to you why I ain't want you involved." Pablo is staring at Mario blazing his mind like a movie on how he's going to murder him.

Bianca comes to stand next to Pablo, "First a thank you would be nice."

Pablo realizes that she's quit talking, "Thank you chica. It was crazy of you, but I'm touched by your action." Pablo leans over and plants a light kiss on Bianca's cheek.

"Thanks, and you're welcome. I just had to be highly pissed off when I had been duped at Shawna's. There was no problem with the count, it was all there. So Cheryl is driving me to my house. The light bulb went off in my head and this happened."

"Okay and how exactly did it happen? Considering you haven't changed clothes or anything since I left you at Shawna's."

"After Cheryl dropped me off, I got right in my car and headed to find you. At the turn off to Windsor Road I see this fool trying to holler at some chick. So I pulled in and took his attention and that was all she wrote." Bianca is smiling like the Cheshire Cat.

"How did you know it was him? You didn't know him at all. Or at least you said that to me the other day. So if it's-"

Bianca cuts him off, "Slow down before you say something stupid or that you end up regretting. I never told no one this and it stays right here, between us. I have a photographic memory, I figured it out when I was 11."

"Are you serious right now? If you have a photographic memory how come you don't do something legal? Wait, how do I know that you're for real? No disrespect intended, it's just-"

"Pablo you're on the verge of pissing me off being sarcastic. If you noticed how I glanced at any paper, picture, or number while you sit and study for hours. I've never lied to you and don't plan on starting to do so now!"

Pablo pulls out his wad of money and takes a $50 bill, "Okay. Imma show you this and you read off the numbers." He shows it to her and for at least five seconds she turns around and repeats every number front, back, and random. "Damn chica, my bad, seriously."

Bianca turns back around, "Look me in the eyes and tell me that you doubted me. Tell me you'd think for one second I would cross you. Tell me you don't trust me. I'm your down ass perra no matter what! I was there for you through everything! So look at me and tell me that you think something crazy!"

"I can't do that, you know it too. If I ever for a second really thought you'd cross me, we wouldn't be standing here talking. Again thank you. Now I have to handle this fool and find one more before the grand finale. I owe you." Pablo pulls Mario out of the porta potty.

"You don't owe me anything. Just don't pull any stunt like that again. Deal?" Bianca puts out her hand.

"Deal." Pablo takes her hand in his and feels a current run up his arm into his chest, brain, and heart. If this is what he's thinking to himself. Pablo drags Mario around the front of the house. "Chica put this shit in my car for me." He hands Bianca everything except one grenade and the nine. "You ready to have fun punk muthafucka? Wait, you can't talk right now." Pablo starts to beat Mario relentlessly, raining kicks to his whole body starting at his ankles working up to his head. He steps back and starts muttering, Bianca is close enough to hear Senora de los Sombras.

Pablo walks to his car and opens the trunk to pull out a gas can. He walks back to where his prey is bloody and broken on the ground, barely breathing. Pablo takes the cap off to pour gas on Mario's body before recapping the can. He then calmly walks back to his trunk to place the can back. He shuts the trunk lid and goes back to his work. "See here you bitch made puta. You are about to go meet mi esposa, nah not Alejandra. La Dama Poderosa, the Powerful Lady. I understand how BB entices your bitch ass. Joey and Juanita too, that's why they're dead and Carlos bitch ass next in line." Pablo lets that sink into his head.

Bianca tells Pablo, "Come on, someone just turned out their driveway and if they happen to have seen us down here they could call the cops."

Pablo acts as if he didn't hear her, "Media, you all fucked up when you crossed the street to play with me on Santa Murete playground. None of you muthafuckas built for this life, it's not in your blood. I let BB eat! I let y'all eat! Even though I didn't f with y'all! On the strength of BB and he got you in this predicament! Life for life! Breath for breath!"

Pablo bends down and lights Mario on fire.

Whoosh!

He jumps back so he doesn't get singed by the fire. "That's how you roast a snake." He walks off with Bianca, "Meet me at my house."

"Okay. No, I'mma follow you to your house."

"Whatever. Watch this Chica." Pablo pulls the pin on the grenade tossing it over hand where Mario's dead body is still burning.

Kaboom!

The corpse flies in the air burning with Pablo laughing crazily.

CHAPTER FIFTEEN

The next morning Pablo and Bianca are riding in his GLC down Pennton Avenue and he spots Carlos in his Chevy SS parked on the corner of View Street. "There's that bitch ass punk Carlos! See that orange SS right on the corner of View Street? Chica switch with me!"

Bianca doesn't hesitate as she takes the wheel while Pablo slides her over his lap into the driver's seat. "What do you want me to do?"

"Turn on Kentwood and swerve around behind him. I'ma kidnap this fool and get some more answers." Pablo gets his nina ready.

Bianca says yes and she asks, "Where are you going to take him?"

"Out to the river, I'm testing his skills at holding his breath. So we'll go out to Waterworks, this time of day nobody should be out and about."

Bianca stops right behind Carlos's SS and Pablo leaps out reaching the passenger door before Carlos can retreat. The chick in the front seat screams as Pablo yanks her out, throwing her to the ground. When he is in the car he places the 9 to Carlos's head. "Nah homie, don't even reach or I'm splattering your shit right now. Pull off!"

Carlos does as told, "Pablo, listen dawg, I swear-"

Whack!

"Shut the fuck up! Drive this bitch to Waterworks and don't get no idea to do anything. You'll have ample enough time to talk. For the record you are not and I'm not your dawg. Now drive bitch!"

When they pull up to the empty lot at Waterworks, Pablo has Carlos park in front of the boat dock. Bianca parks next to the SS facing out. Get out my side. Waterworks has a dock above the Catawba river, it has a boat dock to let the boats down into the water. It is surrounded by trees with walking paths through the woods. People boat, fish, and swim there in the river. The Catawba River also runs into Wateree and Santee Rivers, it's 538 Mi long. Plenty of water for Carlos.

"Pablo, what do you want me to do besides watch out?" Bianca asks. "Come zip tie his hands behind his back for me chica. Then just stand back and look pretty in that pink Fendi sweatsuit."

Whack! Whack! Whack! Whack!

"Don't say another muthafucking word!" Carlos lays still bleeding as Bianca zips the tie around his hands.

"All done. Look, you know he's going to lie so why not just feed him to the gators and snakes. You shouldn't waste so much precious time on scum." Bianca says walking over to sit on the trunk of the GLC.

Pablo drags Carlos over to the water's edge and drops him face-first. Carlos rolls over and sits up on his knees. "Listen I am telling-"

Whack! Whack! Whack!

"I already told you once, I won't again. Now let's play a game, are you ready to play? Yes or no!"

"Yeah, just-"

"Nah nah. Not so fast. First question is, what is Michelle Obama's whole name?" Pablo tucks the nine on his waist knowing he doesn't know.

"Man, how am I supposed to know?" Carlos asks.

Pablo grabbed him by the neck and used the foot of water to push Carlos paste under the surface. He holds him under for 15 seconds before bringing him back up for air. "Wrong answer. It's Michelle LaVaughn Robinson Obama. Next question, what year did LeBron win Rookie of the Year?"

"2004. What's with these questions?" Carlos asks and Bianca wonders the same thing, even though it's sending a chill up her spine watching. "I'm letting you know if you answered wrong under you go, if you answer correctly we move forward. ¿Comprende?"

"Yeah. Just ask me something that I know the answer to."

"See how fast he learned chica?" Pablo asked, looking over at Bianca.

"Yeah. He is a quick learner, guess he can't hold water!" She cracks up laughing.

"Who all did BB involve or was it just the four of you?"

"Just us, I'm serious about that. I don't know who he got the job from." Pablo puts him under the water holding him for almost a minute before pulling him up. Carlos is coughing and spitting up river water.

"Who did he get the job from? Y'all to old is talking more than I cared for, going silent when others walked up. Last time I'm asking."

"I don't know-" Pablo dunks him again and when he brings him back up he is throwing up water. Pablo undoes the tie binding his hands. Putting the 9 to his head. "Swim bitch."

"What-cough-cough"

Boc!

Pablo shoots him in the leg, "Swims across, if you make it you live." Carlos starts swimming and Pablo walks to Bianca, "He goes under before he makes it a quarter mile. That's two miles across."

They get into the GLC and smoke a blunt watching through the back window as Carlos goes under, comes up and goes back down. This happens three times before he doesn't come back up.

"See, all Mexicans can't swim Chica. Least I gave him a chance."

"Yeah, but he did tell you who BB got the job from." Bianca pulls out with Wayne Wonder "Enemies" playing.

"Nah Chica you are wrong. He gave me the answer in his silence, it's only one or two people to be able to invoke that type of fear in someone like Carlos. Think about it and you'll see the light." Pablo lights another blunt. Shit is fixing to start going south he thinks.

"So what are we gonna do then if you know?" Bianca turns out of Waterworks.

"We're gonna keep doing what we've been doing and let the last snake come out. Either I'll end up plotted or in jail, watch and see. I can see it unfolding. The shit was planned the whole time." Pablo cuts up the music and thinks that people can not always stay in darkness. Bianca shows him a text from El Diablo:Meet at Needs & Things:

Bianca pulls into the parking lot of Needs & Things, she parks in the rear of the parking lot. She has the GLC facing Prospect Street. El Diablo hasn't arrived yet, Pablo is smoking a blunt of Orange Octopus and Dubai Green mixed together.

"Chica, listen, I don't know how everything is going to play out in the end of all this mayhem. So on that note I have a small key to give you." Pablo reaches into his pocket and pulls out a small key, the one he had hidden under his sink.

He hands it to Bianca. "What is this key for? I know it ain't no house or car key. What am I supposed to do with that?"

"Shawtie, there's a lot of behind the scenes scheming going on and you are the only one I can trust with it besides Alexis. If I'm wrong please tell me now." Pablo inhaled more smoke, thinking Alexis in his mind.

"You know I can't and thanks for saying what you just did to me. I promise whatever it is I got your back and will for every moment of forever. I'll never fold or crumble down on you." There's more but she doesn't say it out loud. Timing.

"At the hideaway spot I got over on right Street it's the dual apartment on the corner. The only people other than you that know about it are Alexis and my brother. You go under the spot by the trap door under the washer in the kitchen. The box is small, but when you open it with that key, do so with Alexis, then you both know what to do."

"What's inside and why not give the box to Alexis from the jump? I'm not changing my mind or nothing, I'm just asking." Bianca says.

Pablo throws the blunt roach out, "Because Chica, it's gonna take the both of y'all to make it work out to give me a chance. If by chance I get planted it won't matter. This is for if I end up in jail for knocking Carlos, Joey, Mario, Juanita, or BB off. Do I still get your word?" Bianca stared at Pablo right in the eyes, "I'll never fold or crumple down on you. If you get planted, somebody or a lot of somebody's coming with you."

"Thanks, Chica. There's El Diablo, let's go." To see the snake. Pablo says to himself. The memory of his sole mission has come back.

CHAPTER SIXTEEN

El Diablo didn't show up, it was one of his many body-guards. He gave Bianca two envelopes and left. One contained info on their next job which is in St. Louis. The other one was for Bianca and she went pale as a ghost. She wouldn't show Pablo any of the contents, and said she would later.

They drove in silence to her house, even though Pablo tried to start a conversation a few times. When Bianca pulled in her driveway she told Pablo she'll call in a few hours. Then left the car with the envelope. Pablo shoulda pushed the issue, but didn't. He'll see the contents one way or another later.

Pablo goes to Weston Hill to visit Alejandra's grave. When he gets to her grave he sees that it is being taken care of on a daily basis. He lays the purple roses on the ground and sits down with his back to the marble stone.

He says a quick prayer and sits for a while before he starts talking about his life and everything. He tells her about what he has done, to the exact detail of all he has done so far on his path of vengeance. "One to go and then it's the big omega Shawtie."

Pablo stands up and kisses the marble stone. "I'll be back." Then he leaves Weston Hill with a heavy soul. He does his best to always keep the demons at bay, but not anymore. He's inviting them in for a spell. Once he finishes he'll let them depart.

Soon as he reaches home he goes straight to his shrine, stripping down to his Polo boxers shorts. Pablo starts the Santisma Muerte daily ritual, he has the female skeleton clad in a yellow robe, holding the globe in one hand, the other holding a scythe. (Symbolizes hope and prosperity) The scythe reflects the origins as the Grim Reapress for her. "La Parca" is from medieval Spain and represents the moment of death to cut a silver thread. Also that it can reach anyone, anytime, and anywhere.

Pablo lights a red candle, "Señora de las Sombras protect my loved ones here and gone. Guide my heart to the one you've chosen for me." He then lights a blue candle, "Señora de las Sombras guide me into wisdom and heal my sick ones and give all of mi familia y unos amo health." He lights the last candle which is black, "Señora de las Sombras protect my loved ones against all enemies. Against any magic, any harm, and protect me in my quest of murder. Mi corazón es tuyo."

He sits in silence and then recites, "This I ask of you, my most Holy Saint Death of my life, whole surrendering my full devotion to you. So may it be, with your blessing. Please stay with me and keep me with you at all times. Amen."

After Pablo finishes, he washes up and packs a bag for St. Louis. He texts Bianca. :I'll be there in thirty minutes. You okay:

Bianca texts back. :The door a be open I'm packing now:

:Yeah:

Pablo pulls up in his Celica, he had Sergio autumn candy with blue scuro and autumn leather inside. He gets out walking up to Bianca's door wondering how he's gonna get outta this mess.

He walks in to hear the shower running. So he goes into the kitchen for some apple juice. He notices on the white onyx formica the envelope that Bianca wouldn't let him see. The urge to open it is on high, but he just can't bring himself to do it.

After getting the juice he turns around to find Bianca standing in the entry to the kitchen. Miu Miu eyeglasses, guess blouse, and shorts rocking Sergio Rossi heels. "Why didn't you take a peek?"

Pablo opens the apple juice and takes a swallow, "Not my business. If you want me to know or see you'll let me. Plain and simple."

Bianca walks over to the envelope and picks it up. She hands it over to Pablo, "Look inside and when you're finished I'll explain."

She turns and walks out the kitchen. Pablo opens the envelope, dumping the contents on the counter. He drinks the rest of the juice while flipping through the pictures. He counts 12 pictures, each of a man, but in different areas and times. Then the paper holding all the info on the mysterious man.

Pablo walks out and finds Bianca in the living room with her bag ready to leave. He sits down next to her, "Who is that? Because I know for a fact you said you killed your first boyfriend."

Bianca shakes her head and throws her glasses across the room. "I slit his throat myself, there's no way he came back from the dead! There's gotta be some explanation."

"Walk me through the whole story Chica and don't leave any detail out."

She goes on to explain everything and 20 minutes later when she is done Pablo takes her face in his hands, "Chica when the dust settles I got it all under control for you. At least I'mma let my bitches bark for you."

"Alright. Let's handle the job and discuss this later on. So have you talked or heard from BB?" Bianca asks to get up. Switching topics.

"Nah. Fool text a few times, but he is ducking that talk. I ain't sweating it, he gotta come home sooner or later. If not, I'll be going up top to NYC." Pablo gets up walking behind Bianca out the door.

"I'm thinking about stopping after the St. Louis Job." Bianca tells Pablo as he backs out her driveway. He hits the brakes and puts the car into park.

"What? Chica what's up and where did that come from? Wait, I know left field." Pablo is not so much pissed, he's surprised.

"I've been thinking about it for a while now, it's just that there are a lot of things I want to do. Certain aspects of my life and there's no way I can do what I'm doing. I'm just tired of this and wanna live a normal life."

Bianca looks at him for understanding. He gives it to her through his eyes.

"Chica, whatever you wanna do, do it because no one can stop you. There's no way I'm going to sit here and try to talk you out of it. I got your back if that's what you really want. At the end of the day I'm almost done with this shit. I got daughters to raise, family that needs me, friends that depend on me. Your choice." Pablo pulls off.

"Thank you for understanding and I'mma rock with you till we are under the rocks. Can I ask you a question and no it's not that type. How come Alexis isn't your homeboy's lawyer?" Bianca asks.

"Alexis can't defend him because the last time he was on a murder beef. Before you ask, she was told by the judge that she could never defend ButterStreetz again or she'd be barred from practice." Pablo explains.

"What happened? Can't she help his lawyer indirectly?"

"She tried to help his lawyer, but she refused to use anyone's advice. She hates other lawyers and threatened to go to the state bar if Alexis didn't back off. For what happened, it's not my place to tell. You can always ask Alexis."

"It's cool, I was just wondering. Our flight is on United at CDI. Stop at the store real fast." Bianca says to Pablo pointing at the Shell. Pablo swerves in and fills the tank while she's inside. On her way out a skinny white dude is talking to Bianca and pointing his finger and then grabs her arm. Bianca pulls away and keeps walking with the dude right behind her. She spins and stabs him twice in the stomach. Pablo runs over to where the dude is holding his stomach, blood seeping over his hands.

"Chica get in the car and be ready when I come out!"

Pablo takes off his Fendi shirt wrapping his face. Luckily he has on a long sleeve too. He rushes the store, puts his nine in the clerk's face, "Where the video?" When he exits a minute later he stops by the white dude on the ground. "Shoulda let her alone."

Boc! Boc! Boc!

When Pablo jumps in, Bianca peels out of the Shell parking lot. "Thanks."

"No problem."

CHAPTER SEVENTEEN

Bianca and Pablo arrive in St. Louis around 11:45 p.m. It's Friday so the airport is busy. They landed at Lambert, due to them going into the city and Bianca says this won't draw attention. They pick up their bags that have clothes they will only use once while here. "So, where are we staying? I've never been to St. Louis, except through Nelly songs."

"We'll rent a car of course and drive to the outskirts of the city. We should be able to find a hotel room over on Page Blvd. It's not far once we hit the 170." Bianca says in her angelic voice. She is wearing a green tank top that is showing her breasts and nipples off really well. The pair of Levi's is super tight as if painted on her body. On her feet is a pair of gray vans. The perfume she has on is the new Saint Laurents. The smell is intoxicating, it's smell is indescribable.

"Cool with me, I'm just ready to do what we came to do and get ghost like Casper. I'm ready and itching like a crab on nuts to get started on your thing."

"I know and we will soon. Jefe has the things needed for us at an apartment on Arsenal Ave. Hell of a name huh?" Bianca smiles, showing her beautiful fangs, the diamonds shining.

"Yeah, Chica. I'mma go chill out front while you rent the ride. Swing around and pick me up."

"Alright." Bianca walks off to the Hertz desk as Pablo steps outside into the crisp breezy night air. It's chilly, but he's dressed to stay warm in a Jordan running suit with the 4's on his feet. While he waits he texts back and forth with Alexis.

After about ten minutes Bianca pulls up in a '05 Toyota Camry. Pablo puts the two bags in the trunk and slides in the passenger seat. Everything is custom and smells like it just got wiped down with armorall.

"Shawtie, let me ask you something serious and personal?" Pablo glances out the corner of his eye to catch Bianca's reaction. She has a little smile.

"Sure. Only know I get to choose if I want to answer. Also, I get to ask you something personal. Deal?"

"Deal. What are the most important qualities that you look for in someone you date? At least 3." He's looking at her and he can see the wheel turning in her head.

After a couple minutes Bianca answers, "Loyalty. Honesty. Trust. Now the same question to you?"

"Loyalty. Trust. Understanding." Pablo spits them off as fast as a snake spitting venom. "Next question."

She thinks for a moment, "How old were you the first time you had sex?"

After she finishes cracking up, damn near wrecking the car he tells her, "I was 12 and the girl's name was Veronica Diaz. It happened in a treehouse. What about you?" He sees her blush by the lights that are passing their car.

"I was 17, it was with the guy I killed for cheating on me. We were alone for the weekend at his house." Her eyes are watery so he asks her a question to change her mind.

"What do you do to settle any difference in a relationship?"

"I think and believe it's best to talk it out instead of arguing. If I feel anger I walk away until things are calm and then talk to reach an agreement. Communication is key to any relationship. What about you?"

He thinks for a moment before answering. Because he doesn't want to expose too much and he wants his words to come out correct. "I also believe that communication is the number one key. Without that you have no way to build the relationship. I don't like to argue, but at the same time it is good to do so every now and then. Plus the make up sex!" Pablo laughs.

"Just like a man, sex gotta be involved somewhere." Bianca is laughing and they both laugh a few more seconds.

"Nah, Chica, it's a lot to do with love. Sex has been proven to influence how we behave and feel in life, family relationships, school, the workplace, and in our community. Sex defines our attitude about love."

"You're making this up. You gotta be, or you've been watching too many talk shows!" Bianca says this dead face as she pulls into a hotel parking lot. Pablo looks and sees it's a Regency.

"I'm dead serious. The relation between love and sex is complex yes. Yet love wouldn't exist between man and woman without it. Sex can happen without love, but the love builds with holding hands, hugging, kissing and then intercourse. Shows the deep intimacy." Biacna is already parked and staring at him as if he's some other life form.

"Pablo you should be a love or sex doctor due to what you just told me. How, no, where did you even learn that or get that belief?" Bianca asks and she's not making a move to get out the Camry so neither does he.

"Chica, I was locked up for a minute and I read a lot of books from the dictionary to world books. A lot of stuff I just happened to retain in this brain of mine. Know I'd never shoot you some nonsense, I really like you Chica. Real talk." Even though I truly know your agenda Pablo thinks.

Bianca says, "Okay. Let's go get the room, we need our rest. Plus we need to refuel and come up with a plan for tomorrow." She grabs her purse and gets out of the car.

He gets out and follows her in to get the room and picturing in his minds eye about how the sex gonna be between Bianca and him.

CHAPTER EIGHTEEN

They're in the rented Camry traveling down Jefferson Ave. They just came from the connection on Arsenal Ave. and are headed to St. Louis University.

Last night after Bianca got the room, she went out and came back with some shrimp fried rice and eggs. They made small talk, yet she avoided going back to any serious talk with Pablo.

The job out here is to take care of a Professor who raped a student back in the 80's. Then twice in the 90's, and one just recently. The families all took money instead of reporting the acts. Now, it has come time for the Professor to man up and take his beef. It's actually gonna be quite easy considering they have a copy of the Professor's schedule.

"You sure you're gonna be able to lure him away from the school? I don't want you getting caught on video?"

"I got it, trust me. Don't I always come out on top? I got a disguise anyway. Check it." Bianca reaches into a red bookbag and pulls out a red wig and places it on her head and throws on a pair of fake glasses. "White folks call them personality glasses."

"You actually look good. Plus your outfit is tighter than a condom on a dick!"

Both of them laugh as he pulls into a parking space reserved for a teacher. "I'll be back in a few minutes, wish me luck." Bianca slides out with the bookbag on her shoulders.

Pablo hates seeing her leave, yet loves watching that ass in tight jeans. The creator knew what he was doing. Pablo slides on a pair of Oakley's and pulls his fitted Ram's hat down to cover as much of his face as possible. The students aren't paying him any attention whatsoever as they come and go class to class. He starts texting Alexis.

He waits about 20 minutes before seeing Bianca walking with her arm through Professor Andrew's arm. He also notices the 22 she has pointed at his side. It's well hidden, but Pablo knew it'd be there so it wasn't hard not to spot.

Bianca and the Professor slide into the backseat. "Ready."

Pablo backs out slowly and drives off without speaking and as soon as they are out of the campus' sight, the Professor goes night night from the couple smacks of the 22 in Bianca's hand. She pulls out a zip tie and takes care of his wrists and ankles and hops into the front seat next to Pablo.

Pablo takes a left on Delmar Blvd, "So, what you'd say to get the Professor out and walking?" He asks.

"Easy. I walked into his office and told him I needed help on a term paper. Before he knew it the gun was in his side." Bianca smiles, taking off the red wig and glasses, tossing them back in the bookbag.

"So, where we going to handle the Professor. You have to type in the location in the GPS."

"We're going to Forest Park, which is right down the road. Let me take care of it once we get there. Don't get out of the car and as soon as I'm back in you just drive off." Bianca reaches into the glove box and pulls out a piece of cardboard with a string rope through it.

"Chica, a park has a lot of witnesses. Plus it's broad daylight. You know you're taking a big risk and it's not what you're supposed to do. If El-"

"I don't give a shit period! Fuck what El Diablo said to do! As long as he is killed that's all that matters. Let me handle it okay?"

He looks at Bianca and he's never seen her face like it is except on that rooftop in LA. So, he just says, "Okay." Bianca is his partner and it's her call, so let her do her. If shit comes down on us, I'mma let mine rock and that's gonna be that. No questions asked, Pablo thinks to himself. Pablo pulls up and watches Bianca pull out Professor Andrew's from the backseat.

The cardboard has 'I'M A RAPIST' written on it and she places it around his neck, then let's him drop.

Boc! Boc! Boc! Boc! Boc!

Bianca sends her shots right to his face eliminating any way to I.D. the professor that way. She jumps in and he pulls off and then takes a right onto Union Blvd and then a left on Delmar Blvd to get like casper out the city limits.

"You good Shawtie? Seriously?" He asks due to her face being paler than usual. This shit different when playing on this side he thinks.

"Yeah. I'm good, I just can't stand any man who is a rapist. It doesn't sit well with me." Bianca tells him as she leans back into the seat.

Pablo continues to drive around taking this turn and that until arriving at the airport. They're flying right back out even though they don't consider it to be a very wise thing to do.

Pablo is also thinking about Bianca doing what she did even though he knows, sorta knows the why. His reason could be off, maybe one day he'll ask in casual conversation. Until that day arrives Pablo keeps those streams of thought to self.

CHAPTER NINETEEN

L a comida está bien." Bianca laughs and continues, "For real, this food is excellent. I had no idea that you could even cook. I mean not like this here."

"Of course I can cook, I don't eat out all the time. Ask Alexis if you think I'm bullshitting. Plus I have to know how to whip up a decent meal when I have my two rugrats. Wait until you taste the rest." Pablo is standing in his kitchen finishing the dinner he promised Bianca on the flight back from St. Louis.

"I better stop picking little pieces or I'm not gonna be able to eat when you're done. I find it sexy when a man knows his way around a stove."

Bianca has on a blue pair of shorts by Ralph Lauren, a purple long sleeve also by Ralph Lauren, with a pair of Born Emmy Wedges. Her hair is on curls with red highlights. The only jewelry is a silver best friend pendant, he wonders who has the other half.

"Yeah, well if you find it sexy come across the counter and tear off this Hugo tracksuit!" He laughs and she starts up too.

"Just so you know all this food is something out of my recipe book. I collected them for the 5 years I did and tried them out from time to time."

Bianca smiles, "Do you ever burn the food?"

"It's happened, I mainly make the desserts for my girls. Do you enjoy cooking?" He asks Bianca as he scoops out the last of the pineapple chunks. Bianca takes a sip of her red wine, "Yeah. I especially do it during the holidays when I'm visiting the family."

He moves the dishes off the ceramic counter to the table that's placed in the corner of the kitchen-dining room. It's an oak table with 6 chairs that are made of the same oak. It has 2 Dora the Explorer placemats and 4 green placemats. He places the food on both of their paper plates.

"Are you really using paper plates? Why?"

"Yes. I do it because I really don't like washing dishes. If you would like, I'll pull out real plates."

"No, it's okay, really. So what is all this?"

He points at the first thing on her paper plate, "That Chica is sausage, pineapple, and pepper skewers. That second food item is a summery chicken salad. The dessert is a creamy raspberry refrigerator cake." Pablo sits down after placing some of the food on both the plates. "Dig in."

They eat in silence for a few minutes, the sausage and pineapple hits their taste buds like a firework being set off on the 4th of July. The juice from both, mingled with the red pepper puts a sweet, yet tangy taste inside their mouth.

"I truly believe I outdid myself this time." Pablo says.

"This is really good, I mean you could sell this stuff to people. Have you ever thought about opening up a restaurant?" Bianca asks, shoveling another bite of food into her sexy mouth.

"Nah. Because then I could get sued and in trouble using other people's recipes. Plus I got the studio thing that I want to open. I don't see myself opening a restaurant." He takes a bite of the summery chicken salad. He can't say that he cares for it though, so he just chews and swallows like he did the prison food for all those years.

"People use other people's recipes all the time and don't get into any kind of trouble. Besides, if they were printed then they were meant to be used."

Pablo explains to Bianca about the music studio he's opening. How he is going to provide everything needed for the artist, all they have to do is pay for the booth time. He also explains to her how he plans on having a deal with a distribution company to help the artists get the exposure they need in their genre. Plus to allow them to keep their masters and 85% of the money. He only asks for booth money unless signed to his label.

They finish eating and clear the table, throwing away the paper plates. Together they wash and dry the pots and other things that were used in cooking the meal that was just enjoyed together.

"Let's go in the living room and have a drink. Plus catch some TV. What do you say?" He asks Bianca.

She looks unsure for a moment then her face relaxes into a smile. "Okay. Do you have some Brandy?"

"Yeah. Do you want a Corona too?" Pablo asks as he pulls a bottle out the fridge.

"Sure." She answers walking into his living room sitting down on the tan leather sectional.

The living room is painted in Island Green mixed with deep ocean colors. He did this because it makes the room feel as if you're in an upscale resort. He has a Lisbo coffee table that has a cylinder vase with fake violets. Also he has two table stands on each end with Lafayette table lamps. Then a Sony entertainment center with Bose surround sound.

Pablo goes and sits next to Bianca, handing her a Corona and putting the bottle of Brandy on the coffee table. "What do you want to watch?"

"Do you have the movie, The Notebook?"

"Yeah, I actually like that movie. And I find it to be one of the best romance movies of my time." He gets up to find The Notebook and starts it up.

"I won't cry at the end, I promise. So do you watch a lot of romance movies?" Bianca takes a swallow of Brandy straight from the bottle.

"Nah. It has to be really good and not sappy. Plus it has to be realistic, you know." He follows her, taking a drink straight out of the bottle.

"Yeah. Sappy is okay and yes things have to be realistic to be good as well as enjoyable. That's a nice painting of Tahiti."

Bianca is referring to the oil painting that is hanging over the entertainment center. It shows a piece of the island, it's a part of Papenoo Beach that sits on the northern coast of Tahiti. He purchased it from a Laos artist at an exhibit, in prison for 60 books of stamps. Basically $300.

"I've never been, but I will go one day. How'd you like it?" He asks taking another drink, not paying any attention at all to the movie on the TV.

"It was okay, I went for a weekend. The people on the island are so polite. They aren't rude and they are very helpful. Maybe we could go together. What is that painting of?" She's pointing at the one above the fireplace that is catacorner to the TV on the left.

"That's Taipei, Taiwan's capital. It's 101 towers, it sits up above the business district. It's one of the world's tallest buildings. I enjoy the arts even if I only know a little bit. I read a lot to find out about paintings, sculptures, and music. I want to be able to pass along knowledge of the world to my girls and people in the community." He takes another drink.

Bianca kicks off her wedges and pulls her feet underneath her ass. "I find that impressive and a good way to enlighten the children. Opens doors for them and shows that somebody outside of family cares."

Pablo sits his Corona bottle down and leans in and plants his lips right on Bianca's. She pulls away and sits her bottle down. "Sorry, Chica, I-"

"Shh. Come here." Their lips collide together as he goes forward and she goes backwards. Explosions are going off inside both their heads and their ears are ringing. Hands flying everywhere as they undress one another.

CHAPTER TWENTY

I remember the first day that I ever saw you I know that I
loved you when I saw you."

"Shawtie, Gates be going in, real talk. When I hear things I
haven't done, Gates reminds me of Pac." Pablo tells Bianca.

"I only listen to it when you do." She giggles. "For real, he
says things that us women love a man to say." She glances over at
Pablo from above her Fendi glasses.

"Yeah, yeah. I have been hearing that since he first came out.
Anyways, how do you think this meeting with El Diablo is going
to go? I got an idea what it's about." He takes a left on Harper
Ave. Bianca and him are going to meet with El Diablo at the old
retail parking lot on Garter Ave. They are cruising in her white
on white Maserati.

"I think it pertains to what happened in St. Louis. I honestly
don't care, but I'm not going to play dumb or jepordize the moment. I'm honest to Dios, tired of this life. I have plenty of money,
la casa, a couple cars, soon a business, and excellante vida amor. I

don't want to lose any of it by going to jail or ending up dead." She squeezes Pablo's leg where her manicured hand is resting.

"Chica, I overstand and know that you can stop anytime. I told you I got your back. I too enjoy and love my life at the moment. Know also that soon I'm stopping no matter what. Actually and hopefully after I handle that situation with BB and yours."

Bianca clears her throat, "We are going to handle the situations together. I'm going to stop working for El Diablo today. I just pray that it goes over smoothly."

"Chica no matter what he decides, when you tell him he has to agree. My ladies bark for you on whoever and whenever! I'm not saying I'm the baddest, toughest, or meanest on this planet. There's no option of giving caskets for you, especially if somebody disrespects you."

"I know and it's the same for you. So changing subjects, what are we going to eat for dinner? I should say what do you want considering you've been feeding me." Bianca giggles with an angelic sound.

"You! That's all I need to eat!" He puts his hand under her Gucci skirt before she can slap his hand away. Pulling his hand back, "Okay, later for that. How about we go grab my girls, hit Alexis, and slide through Bo's?"

"That's fine with me. I see we're right on time as he's already here."

El Diablo is there already, his Denali is all black on 28's. Pablo notices a different bodyguard this time. El Diablo has a pair of combat boots, fatigues, and a black tee. Pablo has to clear the red from his mind's eye.

The bodyguard is dressed exactly the same and he is short, like 5', but stocky as a WWE wrestler. Pablo pulls up in front of the grill on the Denali and parks the Maserati.

"You ready? Chica, I ain't taking neither of my ladies off my waist." He has both twin berettas on his waist band. Both loaded to the gilt. He isn't going into this meeting unarmed. He also has a Draco under the seat.

"Okay, I'm going with my butterfly taped to my thigh. Let's go. Dama beso." He leans in and tongues Bianca for a couple seconds.

They step out their respective sides of the Maserati. They're in an empty parking lot, the building directly in front of them used to be a retail store. It's closed due to low sales. The bodyguard steps forward to stop them and they assume to search their bodies.

"Pepe, está bien. Let's walk and talk, Pepe will follow." Pablo shakes El Diablo's hand and El Diablo kisses the cheek of Bianca and then they walk in a line of three towards the closed building.

Pablo doesn't feel any type of hard feelings towards El Diablo. He knows the role he played and he knows too that Pepe will likely never see him again. He feels absolutely comfortable because he has the ladies on his waist. Plus Bianca is faster than lightning in a thunderstorm with her butterfly. Both are keen on situations that need pistol play and Pablo never hesitates to let iron sling.

Bianca is going to let El Diablo know she is falling back. One thing for sure is nobody's gonna tell Chica how to live her life. Striving to do so is doves flying with no talking, just the po-po chalking a body for channel 9 news. One certainty for either is death doesn't scare or put fear in them. Pablo is listening to Bianca talk to El Diablo now about her falling back. He self talks to himself to focus.

"I've been doing business with you for two years and the money is good. Life isn't for me anymore and the things I ache to do won't get done if I keep living this way I'm living. So with all due respect and with your acceptance I'm bowing out."

El Diablo is between both of them as they start to circle the parking lot with Pepe about 5 feet behind. Pablo's hand is itching like a bad case of poison ivy has landed on it. Wrong word, wrong look, wrong anything, and the ladies barking like a perra in heat.

"Bianca. Bianca. I take good care of you. ¿Si? I make sure that you are protected. ¿Si? I gave you information that I know was very valuable. ¿Si? Pablo has around 22 months to go on his contract, do you see any way to stay just to help him?"

"You are right on what you said and I've discussed my decision already with Pablo. It is my choice and to me it is final no matter what. I'm thankful for everything you've done for me and I will never forget it as long as I live." Bianca stops walking, so they all stop. They're watching El Diablo and Pepe out their peripheral. No one is saying nothing and it kinda irks Pablo to a certain degree. He knows if it goes wrong he can't win a war against enemies unseen. No matter the people on the teams, but life deals fucked up hands sometimes and like Jadakiss say's, roll with the punches.

El Diablo finally speaks after a couple minutes, "Bianca I want you to know that if you need anything, get in touch. I am going to tell you that you were extremely wrong in how you handled the situation in St. Louis. So you owe not only $100,000, but a punishment for violating my order. Pepe will-"

Pablo steps in front of Bianca placing her behind him, "Slow your roll El Diablo! No disrespect intended, we are men regardless of how I allowed Bianca to handle it in St. Louis is on me. So I'mma pay you the bands and take whatever Pepe got to dish."

"Pablo listen-" Bianca tries to speak, but he cuts her off.

"¡Chica callate! We already went through this before, remember?"

Pepe pulls out a Glock 9 and by the time it is up Pablo has both of his out, one glock 17 pointed directly at Pepe and the other clock 17 pointed at El Diablo. If he is going to die then he is going to take people with him straight to the devil and they all kiss him together.

Pepe! Pablo! ¡Pon las armas adentro! A hora!" El Diablo moved in front of Pepe's line of fire, but still in Pablo's double-time now.

Bianca squeezes his arm, "Por favor, Pablo! It's okay, look at the situation and think of how it won't turn out good for none of us. Baby, please!" In her eyes is pleading, yet ready for whatever.

This is crazy cuz no matter what happens, they're ready for whatever. Pablo will go out in a hail of gunfire before he'll ever allow any man to touch a single strand of hair on Bianca's head. He don't give an fuck who it is, their family better get ready to pick out a suit and casket and pay the preacher.

"Señora de los Sombras." Pablo whispers letting everyone know he'll die for his.

Pepe finally lowered his weapon and put it back behind his back. Pablo then lowers his and puts them back in the front of his waistline. He keeps his hands close though just in case. "It's cool for now, tell your boy over there next time he better fire 'cause I will, no matter what."

El Diablo clears his throat, "Bianca please go to the car and wait on Pablo. Our business is through and it's no hard feelings."

"If it's okay with-"

"Chica! Go to the car and wait for me to finish business! It doesn't concern you anymore. It's cool." Pablo says the words kind of frustrated. He waits until Bianca is safely in the Maserati and then asks, "So where and when do you want me to deliver the money and what's the punishment?" He doesn't care because he is standing 10 and not falling 10 up.

"I'll text you a time and place, I don't fully understand why you allow Bianca to pull that stunt in St Louis. It was cocky, packing this gets a person cut. For the punishment Pepe and you will face off with no weapons. Hands, elbows, knees, whatever is allowed until one of you either blacks out or dies." El Diablo tells this to Pepe in Spanish and they walk to where the Maserati and Denali are parked. Pablo hands Bianca both his guns and lets her know what is about to happen.

"Pass me those brass knuckles I got in the console. Also if for some reason it doesn't go well for me, get up out of here. Don't try no Xena the princess warrior shit. Okay?" Sparking a nervous laugh out of both of them.

Bianca passes over the brass knuckles. They're so thin you can't tell they're on his hand. They're small, but work like a charm. "Pepe is smaller so just don't let him grab and wrestle. He looks strong as shit. Dame beso. You better win or I'mma turn into a black widow. I can shoot with the best."

Pablo leans in and presses his lips against her soft, small, pink ones and pulls back. "I got this, I'mma fuck Pepe up." He walked over in front of Pepe and El Diablo. Like two pits they lock eyes on one another knowing somebody about to get crushed out like an ember on a cigarette. Pablo doesn't underestimate Pepe, nor his skills, he learned that in prison. The smallest muthafuckas can turn out to be the cruelest.

"I forgot one small thing Pablo, you're not allowed to hit back for 45 seconds. I have the timer and will let you know when you can fight back."

"I'll set my watch, I trust it. He sets the timer for 48 seconds and slides the one karat out of his ear into his pocket as he works the brass knuckles into the same pocket. Then placing his Diamond Rosary into his other pocket he puts his guard up and as soon as he does he hits his watch to sync with El Diablo.

Pepe rushes in and Pablo moves out the way easily as a frog catches a fly. Pepe turns and tries once more and the same result. He then throws a combo that after the fourth one gets in and then lands one to Pablo's stomach. It doesn't do any good because his stomach is solid from the workouts in prison and he still does them now. The trick is to keep your stomach muscles tight and hold your breath. He lets him eat on his stomach and puts his back against the Denali as Pepe rains hits to his body. He goes back up top and Pablo had to drop an arm due to him damn near breaking the forearm and that's when he places one on his jaw that damn near dislocates his head from his neck.

Pablo drops his guard and that's when Pepe jabs him busting his lips. Then he slammed one right into Pablo's eye and he knows if he wouldn't have moved just a fraction sooner his nose would have been squashed. The next one lands on the same eye and he feels it split open and starts to close up at the same time. He feels his knees buckling and then the watch goes off at the same time El Diablo says, "Palea Pablo!" Amusement in his voice.

Pablo drops his shoulders and bullrushes Pepe knocking the wind out of him and scoops him straight up and down flat on his back. He's breathing hard and can only see out of his right eye. Pablo's jaw feels funny, but he knows it ain't broke because he ain't got a glass jaw. He tries to catch a little breath as Pepe rolls. "Muthafucka! You think this is sweet! Oh bitch ass!"

Pablo brings a knee right into Pepe's lower back as he arches backwards, slams his right hand into his throat and rolls back to the top. He starts raining down on Chico's face left, right, left, right. He knows he's had to connect about 20 before he figured he was out. Pablo spits in his face "Bitch ass can't fade me! I'm breeded to do this! Welcome to the South Bitch!" Spitting on Pepe again.

Pablo stands up and starts walking towards El Diablo when he gets hit from the back right into the Denali face first. Then he's lifted straight up and in the air back flip style landing on a part of his face and chest. Then he feels Pepe arm go and lock on his neck. Fuck this, he not going to out like this, reaching in his pocket only because Pepe has him and both on their side. Pablo slides his fingers in the brass knuckles and when he pulls his hand out he swings it back. Does this, no lie, probably seven or eight times before Pepe's arm loosens and he slides out and takes advantage before Pepe can recover. He sits on top of his chest and makes it rain punches like raindrops in a thunderstorm.

Pablo turns Pepe's face into baby food and blood everywhere. Covering Pablo and him, plus the pavement around and under his head. Pablo stands up and walks to the hood of the Maserati and sits on the pavement with his back to the grill. He needs air like a fish does water, he's leaking blood like the Hoover Dam just busted.

"Pablo, you only have to pay the money and Bianca is free. I'll drive considering Pepe's over with. I see those Knuckles, but hey, rules are meant to be broken. I'll send you a text later on for the money and for your next assignment." If I don't kill you first, Pablo is thinking.

El Diablo gets over to Pepe and picks him up and throws him in the backseat of the Denali. Then gets in the driver seat and leaves. Pablo goes to the passenger side of the Maserati. "Slide over and drive, Chica." He's just getting into the seat good when he goes to the left going out like the power getting cut off to a house.

CHAPTER TWENTY-ONE

W hat is the business? I see you still ain't come home for no visit?" Pablo tells BB into the phone. He ain't even letting him know that he knows, nor letting it be known it's a problem between the two of them. "Man, I'm telling you, there are so many faces up here it's crazy. I am piping a different bitch every night! I might come home in a couple months, I got something real major in the middle right now."

Trust me I know Pablo thinks, crossing out your own flesh and blood to make money with an enemy. Thinking this he asked, "What you got in the mix? If you can discuss it on the line."

"Nah. It ain't that bad, plus you know how the scramble works. I got a sneaker store opening and I should be able to place one in every state from up north to down south. I have a good person backing me."

"That's good and I hope it works out for you. You know I'll buy shoes from your store. Anyways let me jump off here and get back to work. Get at me in a few."

"All right, be easy. Peace." Pablo clicks the phone off and lights up a blunt of Apple. He takes and smokes half of it and puts it out in the ashtray of the Celica.

"Bra what's up with you? For real, no cutting corners on the answers either. One thing Pablo set out to do in life is not ever drag neither of his brothers into any of his battles. They can fight with the best, yet gun play ain't their life."

"Trip just know that I got crossed out by a snake. That I treated like another brother. But now I realize family is all you got when it comes down to honest loyalty."

"That's what I've always told you and I told your ass from day one that you couldn't trust BB! Know all you got is your blood, that a never cross up on you. If you need-"

"Nah dawg! Porno nor you are getting in nothing I got cooking with nobody. You got to be out here for everyone just in case. Feel me? Plus you have a family that needs you."

Trip laughs, "Who do you think we are? Only know how to throw fists? Anyone can shoot and everyone needs you out here too. You have a lot of family and when are you gonna see that?"

"You correct and yet everyone can shoot a rachet. It's the end side that everyone can't handle. I know I got a family and bra, know if it ever comes down to it I'll ask, until then end of discussion."

"Alright. That's how you want it, cool. When was the last time you talked to Porno?" Trip lights a cigarette.

"Shit, it's been a minute. Ever since he got with that leech he has. Plus he down in SC with her and he's been sending his phone to voicemail. Because of her being so nosy. Catching him is like fishing for a Megalodon." He starts laughing and Trip joins in.

"So what's up with Bianca? What about Alexis?"

"It's cool, we are kicking it with each other, just not rushing things. You know I don't jump into a relationship. Bianca is different though and she understands me. I know she is on a level by herself and she a Bonnie. Alexis is so busy bra, yet you know we go back to free lunch. Once she slows down I'll bag her pretty ass back!" Pablo thinking how Bianca goes harder than the real Bonnie Parker did, that's one reason he kept quiet about the sniper on the retail lot roof the other week. He wasn't a threat to them.

"That's good, and how everyone, even the girls get along and like both of them. I honestly want to see you chill and settle down. Not on no baby shit. Look I got to go get ready for work, bring my nieces over soon so I can see 'em. Call me later."

"All right." They dap up and Trip gets out Pablo's whip and goes inside his house. His brother is married and has two sons. He is a good dude that played with the other side when he was younger. He got straight before he could go crazy and had the same job bouncing for 4 years at Yesterday's then when it closed over to Dolls.

Pablo pulls out his driveway sparking the other half of the blunt turning on Chester Road with his speakers blaring Kevin Gates song "Tiger." He has been waiting on Tedwell to get in touch with him. That's if his daughter Jessica even told him. Only thing on her mind is probably shopping and dick. Pablo seen the look in her blue eyes that day.

He takes a left onto Morganton Boulevard and passes by social services and the county jail. He stops at the light and on impulse turns right onto Decker and pulls into Weston Hill Cemetery where Alejandra was put in the dirt for eternity. He parks and gets out walking up the little path and takes a couple other passes not walking across people's resting place.

Weston Hill is a small cemetery, privately owned. He would guess around 5 or 6 acres with a standing chapel that fits around 100 people. He also would guess it's only 200 graves at the moment. The sun is just setting and the crickets are chirping like crazy. For some reason he's always felt comfortable in a cemetery. Guess it because he respects the dead and is a devotee of Santa Muerte.

Once Pablo gets to Alejandra's grave, he takes in the nice bronze tombstone with Alejandra Iris Lopez on the stone. Born September 3rd, 1983 rested March 14th, 2015. Beloved by many. Never forgotten. Pablo sits down and leans to the side of the gravestone with a shoulder touching it. The keeper keeps fresh flowers, freshly cut grass and weeded. It's been a couple months since he visited the grave and he tells himself it won't happen again.

"Como Chica. I know it's been a couple of months. Sorry about that. Don't be mad at me, it won't happen again. There's a lot of shit being going on and a lot of things discovered."

Pablo knows to some it might seem lunatic to talk to a person who has left the physical. Truthfully he believes they can hear us and if we are truthful to their spirit that is around from time to time, they'll help us. He unloads everything that he's done since that day at the drive-thru at McDonalds.

Lastly he tells her about Bianca. Pablo says a prayer and rises, placing a kiss on the cold headstone before leaving the cemetery.

CHAPTER TWENTY-TWO

R ight now Pablo is in Barnes and Nobles on Morganton
Boulevard. Bianca is at her house doing whatever. He's
picking up some books for his daughters and a couple for
his nephews. Pablo buys them books every month, reading open
doors and allows the reader to a mind picture show.

He buys kids books, but also gets books that teach too. So far
he has a couple of sports books on great players from baseball and
football. Those are for his nephews. Now he's grabbing a few for
his daughters. He normally purchases books that have been written by women or teenage girls. So they see that a woman can do
anything and never need nobody or nothing to show you different.

Ah, a Rachel Field book, he heard of her and the book he's
holding called "Hitty, her first hundred years" it's about a doll
that is an antique and tells of her adventures. Pablo knows the
girls love this one. The next book taken off the shelf is on Rain's
reading level, it's about Geraldine Ferraro, the first woman to be
chosen as a vice presidential candidate by a political party.

Next he snatches up a book about fighting fish by Maria Valdez. Roxie and Rain are crazy about fish. They have a 10 gallon tank, with about 20 fish. It's a small tank, but he's about to purchase the 70 gallon tank for their room at the house. He's already told a guy at Planet Fish that he wants a few goldfish, flame fish, saddleback butterflyfish, a couple neon goby, clownfish, a blue trunkfish, and lastly a algae fish.

He has a list of fish that got copied off the internet and out of the World Book. Things that his daughter like or are into he strives hard to find out about and get them or buy them if it is possible. Some things money just can't buy. One day he'll get a pool for fish, shit he knows a guy with two gators in a pool.

When he gets to the register and puts the books down on the counter he notices the bad ass Latina working the register. She's about 5'1" and probably doesn't weigh more than a buck o five. Her breast damn near about to pop out her red work shirt. Her face is flawless and the only makeup he sees is some green eyeliner. Her hair is layered to her shoulders.

"Will this be all sir? Did you find everything you were searching for okay?" She has pearly white teeth behind pretty pink lips.

"Yeah Shawtie. And you don't gotta say sir. I ain't that old. Do I look old?" He says with a laugh. He knows he looks to be at least 25 so that's 3 years younger than he is. Pablo's hair is in a temp fade with a fresh line, facial hairs trim to look like a 5 o'clock shadow. He's rocking the hell out of a Rocawear all white hat with a red R, the all white roc shirt and rocawear jeans. He's even got a pair of the S Carters.

She smiles and rings up the books and puts them in a Barnes & Noble bag. "That comes to $48.60. Will it be cash, credit or debit?" He's thinking that Shawtie could pass for young Selma Hayek as he tells her, "That'll be cash." Pablo pulls out a wad of money and peels off three twenties. "Keep the change Shawtie. You still haven't answered my question."

"No you don't look old, you're somewhere in your twenties. I'm just polite and say sir and ma'am to everyone. Have a nice day and thank you for the change."

Pablo starts to leave and changes his mind, "Say Shawtie, what's your name?"

She laughs, "Why are you asking that? I know you got a girl-friend or wife."

He laughs, "Shawtie why you say that? I'm asking your name is all and that's it. No disrespect."

"Tell me the reason you want to know my name? The reason I said what I said was because of how you look, the money, and that car sitting right there." She points out the window to his GLC that's a 2008. Sparkling black paint with the numbers 22 and 14 now. It's sitting on a pair of El Diablo rims that's 24s.

"Shawtie first and foremost it ain't nothing as you thinking. I don't move like that. Just because of how I look, I stay right by the way, the money is just that and the car is just a car. Tell me your name and then we'll move from there."

She waits a few seconds, "Okay I'll tell you my name because what can it hurt. Rosa. You don't get no middle or last, that's how you get stalkers." She starts laughing and when she's done he speaks.

"Nice name and it's a true statement of what you just stated. I'm Pablo. I'm 28. I'm basically offering you a job because of one, how you look, two how you talk so proper. It'll be basical-ly answering the phone, sending stuff into people, and appoint-ments. It'll be a few weeks from now, but it's easy work and way less hours than what you are slaving up in this spot. No mornings either, physical time between 2 p.m. and 8 p.m. every day except Sunday. I'll pay you $525 a week for the first 6 months. You do well. I bump it up to $625. What do you say? She doesn't say shit for like 2 minutes, "First what type of establishment do you run? Because the job is easy to do, but I will not do anything illegal. Plus that's a lot of money for a week. How do I know Pablo is your real name and how do I know you're not trying to sell my body to the sex slave trade? Or get-"

Pablo cuts her off, "Hold up. Check it Chica, I ain't into no illegal shit. I ain't no predator of no kind. I'm opening a record-ing studio and here's my business card." Reaching into his back pocket for one and handing it to her. She takes it and looks at it, studying it to see if it's legit.

"Okay. Sorry about that, but a girl gotta protect herself. Where is this recording studio? Do you have security? Cameras?"

"Check it, think on it and then call either number on the card in your hand. There you'll reach me or my wifey Bianca. If you decide to take the job, it will be safe at all times. That's my word. Later." Pablo snatches up the bag and leaves the bookstore, gets into his car and drives off. Not even five minutes and it's red and blue lights in the mirror. Knowing already who it is, so he just pulled over to get it over with and be on his way.

Tap. Tap. Tap.

Pablo pushes the button to let the driver side window down and faces Detective Johnson looking right into his blue eyes. "What I do now? Will you let me call my lawyer Ms. Martinez to file a lawsuit for harassment!" Saying it cocky because ain't no reason for him to pull over.

"Could you step out of the car please? Keep your hands where we can see them?" This muthafucka is real calm and that's unusual especially when bringing up Alexis's name. He can't get out of the car, not yet. Due to having one of the Glock 17s on him, he looks and sees a county car also and two other officers at his trunk.

"All right. I got you, let me roll the window up." Even though he has the mirror tint he's not letting these law enforcement people find a gun in his possession. As soon as the window is up, Pablo peels off and take so many turns until he's on Harper Avenue headed to Bianca's over on Stonewall, letting the popo get nothin cept dust.

He pulls up in front of Bianca's and sees her Maserati ain't there in the driveway. He tried calling, but didn't get an answer so he left her a voicemail. Then calls Trip letting him know what's up and to keep ma and everybody cool. Lastly, he calls Alexis to come get him so they can handle the bullshit that's going on. He leaves everything in the GLC except $2,000.

Alexis scoops him up 15 minutes after he called. Like Ashanti, always on time. One thing watching television and reading and being through the system taught him was to keep a lawyer. Lucky he has Alexis.

"What did you do?"

"Nada. This cracka just-"

"I'm tired of that excuse Pablo! Just tell me so I know what's in store for us!" Alexis says this with more frustration than anger. So he starts at the beginning leaving nothing out.

CHAPTER TWENTY-THREE

Pablo was taken to the magistrate office in the back of the Caldwell County courthouse and placed on a $75,000 bond. The charges were fleeing and evading, reckless endangerment, armed robbery, and possession of a firearm by felon. The only ones that he'll get hit with are the two misdemeanors. The firearm won't stick because nobody that works as an officer of the law has ever caught him with a rachet. The robbery he doesn't know anything about and the timeline they're using is when he was in LA taking care of that dude Trump.

The bullshit is they made sure to book him in at around 2 a.m. when they know there ain't no bondsman or woman getting out the bed. He already knows what bond company he is going to use. It's owned by a guy they call Gene Baker. He a drunk and won't have to hand money to him. Give him some alcohol and a bitch willing to spread their legs for a few days and it's cool. He only does it for bonds that are 10 bands or less. His brother, Trip a handle it for him, so it be around lunchtime he bounce.

A chick that Pablo knows named Sandra was working night shift sergeant and she booked him in and asked what block he wanted to go to. He got her to place him in the FED block, which is 22 block. The homie ButterStreetz is in there on a state case for first-degree. Pablo gave her a Franklin to put him in the cell with his homie.

So after being fingerprinted, pictures taken and put in a black and white zebra suit, he grabbed a blue mat and bedroll. He kept on the S Carter's, due to the fact that they can wear their shoes or get shower shoes. He's keeping his shoes, Sandra walks him down the hallway making small talk until they get buzzed into 22 block. Past the two secure doors and go to the cell and the door opens. "All right. Thanks Sandra."

"No problem. Be good." She leaves after the door slides back closed. Tossing his bedroll to the floor because his homie got a celly, neither of them ever stir at the sound. Pablo looks and sees ButterStreetz got the lower bunk Pablo walks straight over and jumps on top of his homie, "you dead muthafucka!" He wakes up all the way then and is wrestling Pablo off the top of him. After a couple seconds Pablo tells him, "Chill my nigga! It's Me Pablo! What's good fam?"

His celly done jumped off the top rack, he is about 5'6" 180 lb. Light skin, curly hair, and tatted up. Plus cut like a bag of dope. This dude probably is working out with the homie Pablo thinks. That fool does 70 different exercises in a day. They dap each other up and Pablo stands up off the bunk. "What's good? I'm Pablo Streetz."

The light skinned cat jumps back up on his bunk and covers up. The homie gets up and lights a cigarette, they're easy just as anything else you want to sneak into the facility. Butter and him added Streetz to their names with some others when they started rapping on state. ButterStreetz is 5'9" 210 lb, waves like an ocean, he's cut up like a solid statue and tatted up. He speaks with a teenage voice. He's dark skin and crazy as batshit.

"What's good my nigga? What the fuck you in here for?" He sits down exhaling smoke.

Pablo starts making the jail mat up half-ass because he'll be out this bitch tomorrow. "Detective Johnson tried to get me with some County cops. I give him four tires spinning. So then I called Alexis to scoop me up and they hit me with some bullshit misses, PDF, and AR that I definitely didn't commit. Put me on 75 bands, but Ima use Gene to jump out and then when I go to probable cause that should be thrown, slap out." He sits down on the half made mat and kicks off his shoes and the county top.

"Damn, that cracka is still on his bullshit, locking all the homies up that he can, whether charges stick or not. You know I'm about to go to trial, I couldn't take the cop, Victoria told me to, but I said fuck that! I'm a balls to the walls! Those 12 either going to side with a nigga side with the cracka who prosecuting." ButterStreetz throws the butt into the commode. The cell has two metal bunks, a table with a swing seat attached to the wall bolted and cemented. A toilet with a sink that's metal bolted to the wall by the door. The cell is probably 12 ft by 9 ft. "Yo, you get that bread from Tameka?"

"Yeah, she's been bringing it like clockwork every Sunday. A nigga really appreciate that. Those pics were straight too. I know she said you wanted to come up, but I only allowed her and the kids. Plus I don't want anybody coming to visit and get stuck. All the phone time to them too, I get to State undo get a call. The cell phones don't work here anymore, since about a year ago." He lights another roll up.

"Dawg it ain't nothing with the bread, real talk. I'mma about to get the studio up and running so you need to call I'll set up the record. For real I didn't talk to Tameka since before I got wet up, I just drop bread with a note in her mailbox. What's up with your celly?"

"That nigga cool, he a monster on the workout too. He only had three 45 day sentences and ran wild for some misses, but he got pulled over here because he was doggin niggas out in the other blocks. His name is Nutt, he a mute nigga, but he cool and he stays ten toes with me. Don't sweat that shit with the old lady and sorry to hear about Alejandra. Real talk."

Pablo thinking how it would affect him if he couldn't speak, that's some cruel shit to be born with. He says he is a good person then it's good.

"I know your shoe game is sweet even though they got you in the box. But I'mma leave these new S Carters with you. Did Sandra bring you those 95 maxes with the inner soul chamber? Whatever you need I got you until you get home. He lays back on the mat with his hands folded behind his head. ButterStreetz tosses the roll up in the toilet and covers back up. "Yeah. I sold them to a nigga that came on writ a from Pasatank for $350. Best believe I got what was inside beforehand. I heard through the vine that you blazed up Carlos and snatched Joey then Mario. Plus you smashing that bad bitch Bianca!"

"The vine is correct on that all the way. Truth is I got hooked up with BB's Pop's on taking out predators and BB crossing his pops for an enemy of his pops up in Jersey. My reason for talking them so-called homies out is because BB set that up and he ended up in NY. I'mma get his ass and torture that muthafucka when I do! I never thought BB would play that way into foul territory."

It's quiet for a couple minutes, silence where you can hear water dripping a few cells down. Can hear the mice feet on the floor. That's the reason you put a roll up newspaper at the door. He's thinking his homie passed out when he speaks.

"No offense my nigga, but I always knew BB was a snake. I heard of his pop's and I know he legit with his murder game. Just watch every bitch and nigga in his movement, because killing someone's child does something to a person. I'mma go back for some sleep before they pop the locks at 6 for breakfast. I got to show you something before you leave. Night."

"Night dawg. I'm going to take your advice on that too."

CHAPTER TWENTY-FOUR

P op! Pop! Pop! Pop! Pop! Pop!
"Shit! It's time for breakfast already." ButterStreetz says
getting out the bottom bunk. He gets dressed in the zebra
suit and puts on some black forces. After he brushes his teeth
and washes his face he heads out, then Nutt jumps down and
does the same.

Pablo uses the 3 inch toothbrush that they give everyone and
the state toothpaste. They a sell deo, all kinds of soap, shampoo,
and facial shit, yet they won't put toothpaste or toothbrush on
the list. ButterStreetz does have real hygiene and he could use
it but he ain't. Before he can head out the cell both Nutt and
ButterStreetz are back in the cell. ButterStreetz starts speaking,
"Don't you got static with that nigga Maine? From when you y'all
was over in Burke County?"

Nutt standing in the way of the cell door, ButterStreetz leaning on the sink and Pablo on the table. "That shit posed to be
squashed, we jumped him because of some foul shit he did to

Boss. Then we let the knuckles spark head up soon as we met up at rec. I punished him, he blacked my eye that was all. If he trying to shake, then it is whatever! I don't duck no rec!" He gets up off the table to go out of the cell.

ButterStreetz sticks his hand out, "Whoa! Hold on my nigga. I don't think he wants drama and if so he definitely ain't getting no 1 on 1. Plus I got this girl to lay him in the hospital." He shows Pablo a 5 inch blade that's homemade out of the table in the unit.

"Dawg I ain't being disrespectful or ungrateful, but I can beat his ass blindfolded. Pardon me and I'mma go holler at Maine."

"Nutt go tell that, I mean go get Maine and bring that nigga over here. Thanks." Nutt leaves the cell.

"Butter hand me that girl and go on and hold the door for me. That's all I need for now. I know you right there if I need you. I also know if you go Nutt and others are gonna go, but I got this. Trust that." Only reason he's gonna take the banger is not to be disrespectful.

ButterStreetz hands him the blade and steps out to hold the door for Pablo if need be. "Nigga watch my shoes? I ain't tryna to be washing no blood out of them." He laughs.

Pablo pushes the shoes all the way under the bunk, so they touch the wall. Picking the blade back up off the bed and putting it on the waistline of the county jumpsuit. He places his back against the wall between the table and bunk beds to have the advantage if need be.

The cell door opens and Maine walks in, he's 6'0" 180 lb, chubby side, light skinned and waves. "What's up Pablo?" As soon as he goes all the way in, ButterStreetz puts his back to the cell door. Maine's body language is passive at the moment.

"You let me know. If it's going to be static while I'm here for a few hours you might as well pop now and get it done. I hate when I get snuck." Placing his hand on his waist just relaxing it.

"Dawg ain't no shit between us no more. We shot a fair one so in my book we cool. I ain't on BS no more, I've changed my life. I'm Moor now and all that's past is past. So we cool. No hard feelings." He sticks out his hand for a shake.

"I hear you and just know this. Moor or not I don't trust anything you say and if I ever feel you gonna jump crossways I'm hitting your ass up. I damn sho ain't shaking your hand. On that ride out." Pablo knows Cats get into religion in County, Prison, State, or Feds, but 90% is just to make it and not be alone. He only respects it if it's real. Maine switched every time he locked up.

Maine taps on the cell door and ButterStreetz lets him out and steps into the cell. "I see there wasn't any bloodshed. What that nigga say?"

Handing him the blade back, "Thanks. He talkin about we cool and he on the Moor tip now. I know he is faking at an all-time high. On the street he G, on state a Christian, last County trip he Muslim, we banked him he was Jewish, now he Moorish. I told him he jump crossways, I'mma bang his ass like fatback." Pablo starts laughing.

"Alright. Let's go eat, you eaten? I got the calling card. You need it to call somebody."

They walk out into the dayroom, it's 4 big long metal tables and one square table. It's four showers that have a half of a wall separating them. 1 handicapped. 3 phones, 7 cells upstairs, 12 downstairs. It's about 65 dudes and blue jumpers and 8 or 9 and zebras. Pablo sees a couple cats that he knows and shows respect to them. He gets the tray of grits, cake, toast and gives it to ButterStreetz and goes to the phone.

Calling Trip first, then his baby mama, his mom, and then Bianca. He had to catch everyone on the cell phones due to nobody being home. Trip told him Bianca went to Ann Stover and paid the bond already. She did it before he could holler at Gene Baker. It's cool as long as he jumps out of this bitch. After he does all the calls he goes to play dominoes with ButterStreetz.

CHAPTER TWENTY-FIVE

Bianca picked Pablo up a few hours ago from the county lockup. He already talked to Alexis and had Bianca drop $4,000 off before coming to get him. He let her know he'll give her the 6,000 in a week or so. Knowing when he got to the probable cause that shit going to be dismissed.

Alexis also told him don't sweat it or the money. That also after this trial she's doing, they need to sit down and really talk. They went to Pablo's house so he could shower and handle some stuff. Also making a few calls and now they're on Mulberry Street waiting on Mr. Lucas to come so he can rent this office space.

After about 10 minutes a blue minivan pulls up next to Bianca's Maserati. An older, short white man gets out and Pablo asks him, "You Mr. Lucas?"

"Yes sir. You Mr. Valdez?"

"Yeah." Getting out the Maserati and shaking his hand. He is like five foot two so Pablo Towers over him. He has on a pair of blue khakis and white dress, a pair of loafers. He has spectacles and has Homer Simpson hair.

"Let's go inside so you can look around. The office has been repainted, the letting redone, new Windows, Doors, and new plumbing." Mister Lucas unlocked the door and they entered. Bianca stays in the car eating. The walls have a fresh white coat on them. They walk around checking everything in the office space and Pablo picturing where everything will be placed at. "I'll take it Mr. Lucas only I'll give you $2,500 a month."

"$3,000." Mr Lucas says back to him.

"I'll give you $2,700. That's it, take it or leave it."

"Deal." Mr. Lucas sticks his hand out and he shakes it. "Here you go."

Reaching in his Polo jeans Pablo pulls out a wad of money and gives him $2,700 first and last, then $2,700 for 2 months.

Mr. Lucas takes the money and hands the keys over and has Pablo sign some papers and he leaves. Pablo gets Bianca to come in and shows her around. "Chica, I already got a secretary, I think anyway. I know some people who a model it the way I want. I got you as co-owner and vice president. I already lined up someone for business cards, pressing, and distribution." They're standing in the back part of the office when he puts his arms around Bianca and starts kissing her neck nibbling her ear.

"Boy! Stop before you start something you won't finish." She tries to get loose, but only accomplished spinning around to face Pablo and he kisses her sweet lips. Tasting the peach lip gloss she's wearing.

"Chica we breaking this office in before anybody else fucks in here."

Rubbing his hand on her fat, shaved pussy that's bulging in her apple bottom jeans. He knows once he did that it was like Mario putting the pipe to princess… "Look Geinaright, I want you and your crew to paint Caldwell Entertainment on the wall in front. On the right behind the reception desk. Make sure the desk is open on both sides and got flake specks in it. I want the walls to be painted with the teams of schools around here and the college teams."

"Alright. That's easy, it will take about two weeks to get all that done. We'll match the team colors with the mural for the teams. What about the floors?" Geinaright asks.

Marble in front, push gray carpet through all the offices. What are you going to charge me for all this shit?

Geinaright thinks for a moment and then tells him, "Tell you what, twenty-five thousand dollars for it all and $2,000 bonus if it finished in two weeks."

"Alright. Fine with me, I got you 8 bands and I'll drop you the rest next week. Cool?" Sticking his hand out. He shakes it, "Cool. I'll go to Lowes to get the paint and we'll start tomorrow."

"The paint already waiting to be picked up at William Sherman up in Hickory let me go back here for a minute, stop up front and tell Shawtie to hand you the money." Pablo says walking off.

"Later. Thanks for the job."

Pablo met Geinaright over 8 years ago when he was in County. He was doing County work for a second job due to needing extra money. Pablo walks to the back and talks to Travis. The dude is installing all his studio equipment. He told him to make 3 sound booths, put the computer hookups for everything like beatmass, Fruity Loops, Pro Tools, Etc. Put mixers, microphones, the sound proof glass windows everywhere, have doors to the control rooms, even multitrack recorders, stuff for analog patterns, the correct equipment for overdubbing. All this is going to run him $34,350. He ain't trippin because he got to make it back twentyfold.

Travis is looking out because he owes Pablo from back in the day. Walking back out front to where Bianca is sitting in a single chair, he takes her beauty in. She has on a pair of pink and black Jordans, a pair of pink sweatpants with Pablo's name airbrushed on the ass, a pink halter top that shows her breasts off. You can see her nipples and her flat stomach is blinging with a diamond belly ring. She has no makeup on her face, unless you count the peach lip gloss. Her hair is in the Ariana Grande ponytail.

"Let's bounce chica. Got shit I got to handle and I'll meet back up with you later."

"Alright. Do you still need me to handle the situation of finding some people to pass out those cards?" She gets in the passenger seat of the 2014 AMG Pablo traded the GLC in for it and put a little cash down towards it also. He got to get it dipped and tipped as soon as he finds time.

"Yeah chica. Do it how you want and look in on the old boy and tell him I'll be needing 6 lb this weekend. I want them at $2,500 a piece though. Are you going to my spot or yours?"

"Yours. I got you and I'll have a plate for you in the oven by time you get home. So when will Alexis be done with this trial?"

"I don't know, she never had one this big and it's cameras in that muthafucka er' day. Real courtroom drama television. We are going to get at her, time Shawtie, timing."

"So…"

CHAPTER TWENTY-SIX

N eedless to say Pablo hasn't made it back to his house in 3 days. After he dropped Bianca off he went to the little airport in Hickory and dropped two bands for a flight into Orlando. Rented a 2014 Infiniti QS5. The car is bad as shit inside and out, it's got 328 HP and drives smooth. While he was at the studio he received a text from El Diablo and viola, he's in Orlando. Ain't nothing like the sunshine state.

Dude that he's been stalking drives around in a 2014 Charger. It's cherry red, tinted all around, and has 20 inch Pirelli gumballs. If he was still on some jacking type shit, he'd rob the hell out dude. Pablo can tell by the way he dressed that he got money.

Like 2 hours ago before he went into the Ramada that's built inside the Florida Mall on 45th, he had on all Armani. Pablo has decided that he is going to take all that he owns when he catches him slipping. That plus his life.

Also he got to do this job smooth, the info says dude's name is Michael Zellman. He's a teacher at Memorial Middle School and has intimate relations with boys and girls that are students. From what he read in the envelope he has a wife, no children, they have a house on Magnolia Lake Drive and it has high Tech alarms on the premises. 39 and fucking middle schoolers and he picked out the ones he knows are loners, looking for acceptance, on drugs, and ones that really feel like sex is a way to cope.

The file also told Pablo that his wife is 25 and works at a school in Bonnieville. They both got some kind of trust fund from their parents, hers alive, his are deceased. Pablo actually could have laid him in a casket, but he wants to do it a certain way and when the opportunity arises he's going to strike like a pissed-off hungry tiger shark. Once he goes home it's a wrap.

"I love it/I love it" Kevin Gates ringtone comes through his cellphone letting him know who it is before answering.

"What's good Chica?" He asks Bianca.

"Nada. I'm missing you like a cavity missing candy. When are you coming back home?" Her voice sounds a little sad.

"Chica, listen, you know how business meetings go out of town. I know you probably love to come, but they bore you to death. How's everything at home?" He gets comfortable in the driver's seat.

"I know and understand exactly what you're saying and yes I'd be bored most of the day. Everything is cool here with everyone. I'm just running around making sure everyone is doing their job. I am back at the house for now. Where are you?"

"Thank you for handling everything and are the boxes going to be ready this weekend? I'm at the Ramada waiting for the others so we can play golf with the investors."

"Have fun, I know you hate golf." Bianca laughs, "The boxes will be ready when you get back to be moved out. Is it hot?"

"As an egg in boiling water. Look, I'm going to get off here because one of the guys just got off the elevator. One Chica".

"I'll talk to you later. A surprise too, te amo." Bianca clicks off before he can even ask her what the last part was about. And he's not fixing to call back because Zellman just walked back out and is heading towards his car. He's carrying a briefcase with him and he's got on an all white Armani three-piece with matching shoes.

Pablo pulls off right behind and then follows him out the mall parking lot onto OBT. That's what residents call it, tourists know it as Orange Blossom Trail. School has been over for a couple hours so he's either stopping somewhere else again or heading home. Pablo falls back two car lengths and thinks about how he's going to kill Michael Zellman. As long as he goes home to his house. He's also thinking about what Bianca said before she hung up. Yeah they've been fooling around for a couple months and have known each other for a while. Almost two and a half years, he has love for her all across the board, but he doesn't say I love you too, nobody except family. The last female he told I love you too ended up in a graveyard. Love is very complicated when you think about it. If you love someone in sight, are you truly able to do it out of sight. Most females love in sight and lose it when shit gets rough. With Alexis being an exception.

True, Bianca ain't like most women. He wouldn't even begin to try to compare her to any bitch on the planet. Knowing the things she has told him, explained to him about her past and he respects it. He knows she got him on whatever he needs and desires. Plus she'll murder if he needs it, but what if you was catch a long bid in the state or feds. That's a hard question to even answer. Nobody in the universe can guarantee that if their spouse caught a stretch that they stick around forever.

Shit, it's dudes on lock who were married 20-30 years and as soon as they got a long bid. They wife was sucking and fucking before the ink dried on the sentencing sheet. Then you get females to hold on for a few years before they even start giving that pussy and head away. Then you do have some that ride and hold a spouse down, but they also fucking and say they not, but when you locked in the box you already know. You just know how to not give a fuck, let the pussy go and eat you can't be selfish. Always think of your situation being reversed and your chick locked down instead of you.

Pablo keeps following Zellman and sure enough he goes home to his 3 bedroom 2 bath house on Magnolia Lake Dr. He pulls into the driveway parking right behind the 2014 Honda Odyssey, a pair of twin 2013 Ducati's, a twin silver 2014 Mercedes Benz. Pablo doesn't know what's parked in the garage. He pulls in a driveway a couple houses down that has a for sale sign. Scanning the neighborhood, it's quiet, it's twilight now so he doubts in this neighborhood people will be out late. Plus he feels good because Zellman lives damn near at the end of the block.

He decides to leave and come back in an hour or two, so he pulls out the driveway and takes a right. He takes another right on Edgewater Drive going to a Krystals and grabs 10 small Slammer burgers. At least that's what Hardee's called them when they sold them ordering a bottle of water also. Smashing the food in the parking lot and text Bianca.

:Chica, what's good? Have you heard from that female Rosa?:
:Nah, are you sure she's going to take the job?:
:I'm positive. I threw a lot of money to get her chica. I know she'll be a good fit:
:How you ukt? Udk her from a hole in the ground:
:BC of how she conducts herself when I met her at B&N's. Let me know if you do. Goodnight:
:G.N.T.A!:
He shakes his head and texts Alexis.
:You up?:
:On the way to Dreamland. How are you?:
:I'm good. How's trial?:
:At least two more weeks, this is a draining case. Wish me luck:
:Okay, yet you don't need it. See you when you are free. GN:
:Night ttys & please stayed focused & don't get hurt:
Putting his phone away he pulls out the Krystals parking lot and heads back to Zellman's house on Mongolia Lake. Pablo going up in there tonight, fuck it. He knows exactly how he's going to play it out.

He says a little prayer as he's driving back. Turning onto the street going down to the end and turns around and stops the rental car in front of Zellman's mailbox. It's one of those mail-boxes that's built into the bricks.

He puts on a pair of latex gloves and then slides his hand into some Nike batting gloves. He pulls the skullcap over his head, but doesn't cover his face. Checking the Glock that he bought off the street down by Paramore Avenue from a dread. The clip is fully loaded with 17 shells and that's overdoing it to be honest.

He gets out of the Infiniti QS5 and walks up the driveway, down the little stone pebble path to the front door and rings the doorbell. He can hear the ding sound play on the other side. He rings it three more times and finally the door is answered by his wife. He ain't going to front, the bitch bad even in her bathrobe. Standing around 5', 140 lbs, gray eyes and blondish reddish hair down to her ass. She has sweat on her forehead so he must have interrupted them fucking.

"Yes. Can I help you?" Pablo can see her cleavage and can tell she has a rack on her. He looks at her toes, they are alright. He looks back at her face.

"Ma'am my car broke down just now, it's right there by your mailbox. I was looking at the home for sale a few doors down. Could I use your phone to call for a tow truck?" He said smiling an innocent smile.

"I'm sorry, all we-" Pablo doesn't even let her finish, because he knows this bitch isn't about to let him come into her house. No matter what is said to her. He pulls the glock from his waist and puts it exactly on her sweaty forehead.

"Don't speak another word or your brains getting ejected. Am I clear? Just nod your answer."

She nods her head up and down. He makes her back up into the little entry way, shutting the door after he steps into the house. "Where is Michael at? Don't lie or else."

She points and he waves his hand for her to show him. She turns around and starts walking. She has no ass at all, after a few steps she takes a left and they're in the living room. It is an aver-age sized room and only has a recliner, loveseat, and a four seat couch. It all matches the gray carpet, there's no tables or pictures.

The lighting is overhead and in each corner. At first his ears, nor eyes actually take in what he is seeing or hearing. When he does he pushes Mrs. Zellman down to the floor with her robe coming open and she rolled on her back on purpose. Showing him a set of double d's and a pussy fat as a softball with a set of pink lips and it's shaved clean.

At the center of the floor is her husband Michael, the man Pablo came to kill on top of a girl who can only be about 16. She sees him, but he doesn't nor does he even realize that Pablo is standing there and bringing death. "Uh um!" Clearing his throat.

He looks up and looks shocked rolling off the girl. "W…W… who are you? W…What do you want? I…I have money just please don't hurt us." Pablo only lets him say all that because it's weird how muthafuckas ask for something they can't receive.

"Close your robe and you sit on the couch with Michael. Little girl get your clothes on and don't try nothing stupid and you'll make it out of this house without a scratch."

"I…I… got-" cutting him off by walking over to him and Pablo busts him in the head twice causing blood to come pouring out. roughhousing him up on the couch next to his wife. "P..P.. Please."

Whack! Whack! Whack! Whack! Whack!

Smacking him three more times and his wife twice. She starts crying, he got tears falling also. Not that Pablo gives a shit. "Don't speak unless given permission! Understand? Nod your answer!"

He nods and Pablo turns and sees Shawtie has gotten dressed in a raggedy pair of skinny jeans, an old ass Minnie Mouse shirt, and a pair of white pro keds. She is sitting on the loveseat, not showing any emotion whatsoever. He kinda respects that because most teenagers show some type of emotion. He doesn't know what he's going to do now because the situation is different from what he thought it'd be. Fate is a bitch and dealing the cards tonight. Standing where he can see all three people before speaking again.

"Check this out, I'm going to ask some questions that I want truthful answers. If I feel you are not being truthful, well it won't be pretty. Shawtie what's your name?" He looks at the teen on the loveseat. She's pale as a ghost. When she speaks her teeth are

AGAINST ALL ENEMIES: TROUBLEMAKER

fucked up bad. Plus she can only weigh around 90 lbs. Her hair is dirty blond.

"Betsy Ann."

"How old are you?"

"16, I'll be 17 in 4 more months." She's talking with no nervousness or nothing. His guess is she has been through a lot or just doesn't care one way or another.

"Where are you from and why you up in here doing what you are doing? Also, is this bitch part of it? Don't leave nothing out." He wanna just rest they ass on that couch, but first he needs to know what is really going on. He doesn't know what is up with Mrs. Zellman and maybe she's scared of her husband. He only buys about 2% of that though as it goes through his brain.

Shawtie takes a couple minutes, like she's thinking of what to spill and what not to spill. Finally Betsy Ann answers, "I'm originally from a small town in North Dakota. My parents got murdered a few years ago and I was sent here to live with my grandmother. I met Michael and Kristie at a clothing store. I got caught shoplifting and they paid for the stolen clothes so I wouldn't go to juvie." She has her head down the whole time she's speaking.

"Look youngin, I mean Betsy Ann, I ain't going to kill you. That's my word. Hold your head up when you talk, no matter what this life throws at you. Know the situation you are in right now isn't your fault." Pablo says with total sincerity.

"You're wrong! You don't know anything about me or my life! I steal, I lie, I cheat, I get fucked by older people who pay me, and I get high! So-"

"I know about you, it's way more than you think or believe. I had someone close to me go through the same shit and you can't blame yourself! You're the victim. I'mma help you if you want it, if not, tell me right now."

Pablo looks at her with pain in his eyes that outta touch her soul.

She looks down and back up with glassy eyes, "I don't know you nor if you are telling the truth. That look, looks like the one I see every morning and I do want help. I hate letting them fuck my body and… and…" Betsy Ann puts her head down and he can tell she is crying.

"Betsy Ann go in another room for a few minutes. I'll call you when I'm ready to go, don't make me regret my decision." She gets up and goes down the hall towards the back of the house.

Pablo walks over to the Zellmans, "Both.Of.You.Are.Some. Sick.Fucks!"

He normally doesn't do this, but it's an exception tonight. "Tell me the truth and I will let you both live. I will be watching you both so no funny business. First question, where's the money?"

"It's in the bedroom closet! It's two briefcases with a lot of money! You can have it! Please-"

Whack! Whack! Whack! Whack! Whack! Whack! Whack!

Pistol-whipping Michael a little and he is about to lose consciousness.

"Betsy Ann! Come here!" He hollers for the little Shawtie. She comes into the living room dry eyed and as if she has washed her face. "Do me a solid, go in the bedroom and look in the closet until you find two briefcases and come back in here."

She does as he asks for and within a minute she's back with two briefcases, they're regular ass ones too. One is the one Michael had coming out of the Ramada earlier. He opens one then the other and he hears Betsy Ann let out air, she probably never seen this much money in her life. Shit, he's never seen this much money in his life. It's all $100 bills, fresh at that.

"Kristy how much in these and don't play stupid."

"2.5 million dollars in each one. It's not our-" Pablo cuts her off "Bitch don't add nothing to the answer! Now Betsy Ann take the briefcases to the car that's by the mailbox and wait for me." The girl ain't moving an inch. "Betsy-"

"No! Whoever you are and no matter what you are about to do I'm staying watching! At least give me the satisfaction of that. Please." She is pleading not only with words, but with her eyes and he knows he should make her leave, yet for some reason he doesn't.

"Alright. but you better not tell a soul living and breathing what you see. Are we clear?" Pablo looks at her with fire in his eyes to confer to her that he's not playing.

"I swear on my parents grave. I will take this to my grave whenever that may be." Her facial expression looks to be solid so he's not going to make her go.

"Stand back with the cases by the entryway. Michael, get down on the floor and put your ass up in the air." He slides off to the floor and blood is all over the place he's touching. Michael put his ass in the air, "Kristy, do not for no reason get off that couch. Understand?" He looks at her streaked, bloody face as she nods.

Pablo gets down to Michael's level, "You like to fuck youngins? You got a pretty wife and you still fuck kids. I don't know how long and personally, I don't care, because it stops now! No one will ever have to worry about you touching! Violating their young bodies again! I hope you burn for eternity, shit I'll probably see you one day again!"

He stops talking and does something he hasn't done in a while, he prays to God. Only he does it silently with his head bowed. Once he finishes and looks at Michael's ass cheeks and tells Kristy, "Come here Kristy and open your husband's cheeks for me. Now! You have 3 seconds." She's off the couch faster than expected.

Kristy opens his cheeks and he's begging no, but Pablo ain't bout to ask him how he thinks. As soon as he sees his brown eye he pushes the gun with extreme force into his ass and pulls the trigger twice, he's screaming as Pablo yanks the glock out and shoots him in the back of the head. Kristy falls back against the couch, tears falling like waterfalls. He leans up and grabs Kristy by her hair and yanks her up and pushes her all the way prone to the couch.

"Bitch don't say or make another fucking sound! You are a rapist pedophile just like your dead husband! You got looks and a nice body and any grown man would fuck I'm sure. I know you're gonna say anything to get out of this situation. I'm sorry to inform you, it won't work. I'm not a gullible muthafucka, I'm just a man though, I'mma fuck you right now and you're gonna love it, so lay back spreading those legs and close your eyes while you spread those pussy lips."

Kristy does as he tells her and her head is to the side and eyes shut tight. Pablo puts the shitty barrel of the glock right in her canal opening to her pussy ripping it and pulls the trigger 2 times and then she gets hit once in the forehead, well above her left temple. He drops the gun on her body knowing it's no prints on it the clip or shells. He looks at Betsy Ann, she looks like she's in shock. He goes to her and grabs her arm.

"Let's get out of here before the cops get here! Grab the briefs!" Directing her straight out of the house to the rented QS5 and they both get in, she has the cases on the floor in front of the passenger seat. As he pulls off they hear sirens and can see a few people on their lawns. He takes a left, then the first right, then keeps doing turns. Left, right, left and so forth until he just comes out to an intersection. He has no clue where he's at.

"Betsy Ann, look you wanted to stay and I think that what I did was better than other options. Shake that shit off and tell me how to get to the airport or better yet a low key motel. And before you think it, I don't want anything from you. Only your promise you made back there." He looks at her.

"We're on Colonial Drive, if you turn either way. It's motels all around here. I'm okay, I really am. I'm going to keep my promise and I know you're not like them. Thank you mister, you can drop me off at my grandmother's. I-"

"Nah. Look obviously you ain't trying to be there and if I drop you off you're going to keep up this lifestyle. I can't allow you to do that so what I'm going to do is this…"

CHAPTER TWENTY-SEVEN

Before Pablo let Betsy Ann fly out of Carolina, he explained and ran down a lot of things to her. He talked to her for hours and got a brown envelope and put $500,000 inside of it and told her to send some to her grandmother.

Then together they took $500,000 and spread it to different churches of all faiths in eight different counties from Florida, Georgia, Alabama, and the Carolinas. They even dropped money to some Masjids, one witch covenant, and different orgs of Santisma Murete. Then they took $500,000 more to split it with homeless shelters, soup kitchens, homeless orgs for kids. He also gave some to Red crosses, Salvation Army, thrift shops, Goodwills, and food banks taking another $300,000 doing that. Then $200,000 he split amongst his people, free and locked up.

Betsy Ann helped him a lot and it took a few days, yet he was cool with what they did and it was his own way of helping people in need and not to mention paying penance. You have to pay forward, it's just a part of life.

The other 3 mill was broken between Betsy Ann and him yet he only gave her $500,000. Explaining he got the rest and it will not go nowhere, she has to take care of her people and get her diploma. Learn to manage money, how to deal with having money.

She called her grandmother and explained that she was going back to North Dakota to live with a friend. Really her cousin move small time out there. He's going to help her get clean and stay clean. She promised again to not tell no one about nothing that had happened and definitely not flaunt money. Only use what is needed, he gave her all his numbers in case she needed anything or to just talk and check in mandatory twice a week. When she boarded her flight she had a Louis bag with the money. A few Louis suitcases with brand new clothes. He hugged her and told her to be safe and finish school and that he'd see her soon, but talk to her sooner.

That was over a month ago and El Diablo has had him casket 8 people since that Orlando trip. She has called him every other day and she sounded better. Pablo then since has gave his people 6 ways $250,000 in their bank accounts.

When he went to drop a bag into Tameka's mailbox she actually ran out and stopped him. Informing him that while he was away they sentenced ButterStreetz to life and sent him to Central up in Raleigh. He vowed he gonna get his homie home somehow. He talked to BB a few times, but he putting off the coming home visit like he know something was up.

Rosa took the spot offered to her as a secretary at Caldwell Recording Studio. Pablo even gave her sister Gloria a job doing the same thing, just less money. He hasn't fully opened up yet and it's already booked up for a month.

Pablo has just dropped his daughters back at his baby mama's house and gave her a few bands. She doesn't need it, she hit a rough spot while he was incarcerated, but soon he got released he fixed that. Her ass went back to the straight and narrow. She was very close to being on the receiving end of a bullet, but he couldn't do that to his daughters.

After grabbing something to eat at Hardee's where he chopped it up with Nancy and crushed 2 burgers, curly fries, and iced tea he hit Rosa. Told her he's stopping by her place. She lives in Granite Falls in a mobile home park they called Spring Lake. Her and her sister Gloria owned a three-bed two-bath double-wide and paid for the lot it's on. Pablo pulls the AMG into the little dirt driveway beside their Mustang. It's a 2006 all blue with factory rims.

After getting out he peeps Rosa on the end of the concrete porch in a beach chair with a Corona in her petite hand. Rosa is rocking a pair of Chloe wedge sandals, a green silk maxi dress, a pair of studded earrings and red lipstick. Her long black hair is curled up into a bun, sitting on top of her head. Pablo takes the beach chair beside her, "What's good Shawtie?"

Rosa takes a swig of beer, "Nada Pablo. Do you want something to drink?"

"Nah. I'm cool, thanks though. Listen, I stopped by to speak and ask you a serious question. If you are not cool with it then be honest. If you down with it then you'll be well taken care of and no it's nothing sexual. Just give me your word that it goes no further than your ears." He looks at her with eyes that let her know it's not a game.

"Spit it out. If I don't like what you say I'll tell you. I promise I won't repeat nothing that is said and I know it ain't sexual because you got a wifey. Actual two. Plus, I don't get down like that with a man in a relationship." Rosa takes another sip of beer. Looking away from his eyes because that last part was pure bullshit.

"First, I'm not in a relationship the way you or anyone else thinks. Bianca and I are basically just going one day at a time and we're friends before anything else. Same with Alexis, where's your sister?"

"She's gone somewhere with her boyfriend. So you gonna ask what you got to or not? I don't have all day." She smiles as she says this.

This causes Pablo to laugh, "If I take all day then you'll have all day. Let's go inside, I don't want no nosy ass neighbors overhearing what I gotta say." He gets up off the beach chair and goes up the three concrete blocks that are the steps, opening the screen door and walking right into the living room.

It's a hall to the right and he peeps three doors. The living room isn't big considering it has the kitchen and dining area sharing space. The living room has an entertainment system against the wall. It's a couch right in front of him with a flower pattern and probably holds three people. There's a recliner to his left and the cabinet is behind it, then the stove, sink, and fridge. It's a wooden table with four chairs, he can't believe how small it actually is. He plops down on the couch with Rosa sitting down next to him curling one leg under her opposite thigh.

"Peep game Rosa. I asked you to work for me, because of your voice, the way you speak like you are highly educated. And lastly because you're sexier than a clit above lips! Pardon my language Shawtie. I also did because I need you to help me set somebody up. So I can handle a small matter that I have with them. That's it."

Rosa doesn't speak for a few minutes as she finishes the Corona and gets up and throws the empty bottle in the trash. She then comes and sits back down next to Pablo on the couch at the end. She sits opposite from him holding her leg under her Indian style facing him. So he turns his body somewhat to the right so he can see her better and not have to twist his neck.

"First and foremost, thank you, for not only giving me a decent and high paying job, but also my sister. Thank you for the compliment and don't worry about how you speak. I've heard worse language from people I don't know, what do I have to do exactly? Who is the person? What did they do? Lastly, what are you going to do?"

Ain't no way you can sit in fake it to Rosa what is going to go down. If by chance she goes to the cops he'll smoke her like a cigarette being hotboxed. So Pablo runs it down to her while watching her facial expressions throughout the whole spill. Her face doesn't change at all, which he feels is good on his part. Pablo waits for about 5 minutes for her to answer.

"I've never ever done anything like this before. I never thought to do anything like this before. It's crazy ass shit, but I'm intrigued by what you told me and how you described the plan. Do you really believe it could work the way you said? Is there any doubt whatsoever in your mind?" Rosa ain't showing no ounce of fear or second-guessing.

"Nope. No doubt. Not at all because I know that it will work. All we have to do is stick to what I just told you and it's no way it can fail. $25,000 if you agree." He says literally holding his breath.

Rosa runs her hand over her hair, he can tell it's just a habit. "Alright on one condition though." Rosa holds up one finger.

"What's that?" His mind is running a million scenarios.

"I get to tell Gloria. That way if, and I'm putting a major emphasis on the word if, if something goes wrong she'll know what to do for us."

"Nah. I don't know, I'm still not 100% sure about involving you. No disrespect at all intended, but I barely know you outside of work. I'm taking a big risk with you and I know Gloria even less."

Rosa stands up and drops her green silk maxi dress to the floor. Before Pablo can say anything she turns around and he sees two bullet scars on her lower back. She turns back around and slides her dress back on and sits back down like it ain't nothing. Her body all over is pecan brown. Her breasts sit up with big brown dollar size nipples and her ass sits correct. Her kitty was shaven and her clit pierced. He noticed all that in the 15 second play just now and Chica better be glad he ain't trying to bust her guts loose. Yet. He thinks to himself it's only a matter of time before you bust that kitty sure as Jordan won chips with Pippen.

"Now you've seen all of me, I just showed you two bullet scars. That I received for no reason, other than being in the wrong place at the wrong time. This was out in Cali while visiting my family and some trigger-happy cops came through my cousin's barrio and just opened fire. I'm lucky to be alive, much less able to walk. So this is how you know." Her eyes are watery as she tells Pablo this.

"Alright. Point taken. I'll give you the money before I leave. Here's how we got to do it Rosa." They talk and plan over the next 2 hours.

CHAPTER TWENTY-EIGHT

P ablo is sitting outside MaGuffy's restaurant in Hickory, he's in a stolen 98 Lexus. It ain't nothing, but factory and possibly could stop running at any moment. Rosa has been inside eating with Benny Johnson for over an hour. The detective who caused his homie to get life and has been harassing him for the longest. Butterstreets gave him info on him, that's one of the things he shared with Pablo before he was released from County.

Pablo has no clue how Rosa actually got the Detective to take her out on a date. He has to know she works for him and knowing him, he is doing all this to see if he can gain any information about him from her. Then again he's a man and he's also trying to fuck Rosa. She is a bad bitch hands down all the way around. All Pablo did was explain to Rosa who, what, when, and where and did her thing.

Bianca been acting a little weird after he brought up what she said over the phone while he was in Orlando. She's been kind of distant and he really can't blame her for acting that way. He's playing their last conversation in his head like it was yesterday instead of 3 weeks ago.

They were at the studio overseeing everything when he pulled her into his half-done office. "Chica I gotta ask you about that I love you, that you said over the phone. What's the deal with that?" Pablo leans against the wall and she leans next to him.

"Honestly it just came out, I didn't intend for that. I'm not regretting the words or going to downplay it. I honestly do love you. I only say them words if I mean them. I don't want anything you can't give and I'll take what you can, even if it's just what we're doing now." Bianca looks kind of nervous.

"Chica you know I say only what I mean and I'll never lie or play games on you. I like what we have and I love every minute of it. You got to know that I don't know, nor can I say I love you on that level. I love you on all levels to a certain degree. My daughters like you and that goes a long way. It's just, I'm not ready for a solid one-on-one commitment at this moment. It's got nothing to do with you. Trust."

Bianca literally looks as if at any second the waterfalls are going to start. She's holding it though as she speaks, "Look I understand everything and I love your daughters to death. I get along with your family and that's a plus. I know you're not ready to settle down because of what happened to Alejandra. I do care, but don't care if you fuck some other bitch, just wrap up less it Alexis. Be honest about it and don't play me nor forget who's who and who's for you unconditionally. I love you and that's not going to change."

He folds Bianca in his arms and holds her, letting her know, "Chica, I haven't fucked no other bitch, as of yet, not even Alexis. If I do, I'm a wrap my man up and I'll tell you. I just ain't trying to rush or fuck up a good thing by doing so. Give me time and let's just keep coasting Chica."

Bianca pulls away and pecks his lips, "Pablo. Te amo mucho, mi toda corazón. Nada es tiempo. I'll see you later." She then left and he seen her everyday, but her change is seeable. They have only got together between the sheets twice since then. Like they say men are from Mars women Venus. It's cool.

After another 10 minutes, out comes Rosa holding Benny's hand. They both are smiling, looking as if they're really enjoying their time out together. Benny AKA Detective Johnson has on a pair of jeans, a button-down polo shirt and a pair of Nikes on his feet.

Rosa has her long hair flowing freely to her shoulders. She dyed it light green on the tips. She is rocking a Jolibe Atelier dress that's all black to her Gucci heels. The dress is open down the center of her chest and stomach. It has her arms bare and mid-thigh down is bare. Pablo bought the dress for her and Chica banging out in that bitch to the point Pablo dick rock up.

They get to his car which is a white 2009 325i. That fool taking money from somebody, because he knows that he can't afford that car on a detective salary. It don't matter because after tonight if all goes as planned a car will be the last of his worries. When he pulls out Pablo's right behind him, then he falls back 3 cars.

He drives down 321 then cuts up Jasper Street and onto Milton Street into a driveway in front of a house sitting on Lake Catawba. Pablo now knows for sure as ice melts into water that he can't afford this big ass house on a cop's salary. These houses go a mill easy. Thinking to himself that he'll rob his punk-ass after he's done shaking him up.

Pablo goes to the end of the street and busts a vee and parks at the end of his driveway. It's dark as midnight on the street, the only lights are the few street lights in certain areas and front porch lights.

He waits 15 minutes and takes off out of the car like a rocket pulling the ski mask over his face and pulling the slide back on the 9 to make sure it's one ready.

It's 14 left in the clip even though he don't plan on using any of them. Searching the lining of the roof for motion lights, spotting two so he flattened himself against the bricks of the house and went slowly under them. He takes the corner of the house, he chose the wrong side because now he's going to have to leap the fence. Luckily, he can jump a little bit. Putting the gun deep in his waist and jumping, grabbing the top of the fence and pulling himself over to the ground in the backyard. From what he can see it's clean, and recently cut. There's a boat dock, a mini speed boat. He knows absolutely nothing about boats. The moonlight is sparkling off the water of the Catawba River. Looking up two spotting the motion lights and stays close to the wall.

When rounding the corner he sees a wooden deck that's got to be at least 15 by 15. It has a grill that looks like it could cook a whole deer on it, a table that has at least eight chairs around it and a couple bed looking things. Going to the steps looking directly into what he assumes is the rec room, because you can see a pool table and a couple of pinball machines.

As he starts to go up the steps to the deck he spots sight of Rosa coming towards the French doors. Rosa pushes them open and comes out onto the deck. Pablo drops down and rolls under the deck. Not tripping about being seen by no one, because he's dressed head-to-toe in black. His neck was even wrapped in a black winter scarf.

"Pablo? Pablo?" Rosa says his name loud enough to where he can hear her. He doesn't say anything, he lies still like a possum. "Pablo come on in, it's safe. I know you're back here because I already looked out the front and the car's empty. Come on, I swear it's safe."

He waits a few seconds and then comes from under the deck. Walking up the deck steps with a 9 raised and ready to knock all into the next plane like Kevin Hart.

Rosa standing like two steps out the French doors fine as hell. She doesn't look any different than when she exited the car. Just being cautious and he's thinking she is playing me. "Where is Benny at Rosa? Don't fuck with me, I swear I'll splatter your memories into the air tonight." Stopping about 2 ft in front of Rosa.

"Come look for yourself, I'm not double-crossing you. I gave my word to you and I won't break it. You can put the gun up, because you won't need it. Come on." With that said she turns around and walks back into the house. He follows her, but a couple of feet behind her too, just so he don't walk into no surprise attack. If that's the situation it's going to be a coroner coming out here tonight for more than one body.

When Pablo steps into the room, it is a rec room, 2 pinball machines, 2 video games, pool table, dart board, and an entertainment center. The carpet is money green and the walls have pictures of stars from Nascar to hockey. As he keeps following Rosa she leads him down the hall past two rooms with doors closed, then the dining room, lastly the living room and up some iron spiral stairs to the second floor.

It's four rooms with 3 doors close, the room at the end of the hall is open. It's a dim light inside the room, Rosa steps into the room with him right on her heels and it takes a second for the brain to register what he's seeing with his eyes. When it finally does kick in, he asks Rosa, "What the fuck Shawtie!? This wasn't the muthafucking plan at all! Shit! Shit! Shit!"

Pablo then starts pacing back and forth in front of the king size bed. On the bed is Detective Benny Johnson, with his hands cuffed to the metal ring on the headboard and his throat split open ear to ear like a second mouth. All he has on is his boxer briefs.

Rosa ain't saying shit and it is really pissing him off. He runs up on her grabbing her throat and starts choking her, as he pins her up on the wall with the gun to her head. "Shawtie! What the fuck happened?! You better answer me now or you're going to meet somebody!" Pablo lets her go and backs up because he didn't mean to grab and choke Rosa. He's got to calm down fast and think.

Rosa rubs her throat and looks like she wants to cry, but put him to sleep at the same time. A million thoughts are running through his brain, he never had any intentions of killing a cop. Much less a detective, shit this is going to be crazy as a muthafucking mental hospital when this gets out. He's got to think what to do because he's not going to jail for no cop murder. Rosa is crazy as batshit for putting them in this type of situation. "Fuck it, deal with it the best way possible."

Rosa finally speaks, "Pablo listen, I got him straight up here and he wanted to handcuff me. I told him only if he let me handcuffed him first. As soon as I did I noticed a switchblade on his nightstand and I grabbed it and just let it slit his shit. Fuck him, he's a cop! I know-"

"Chill out! Fuck it! That happened and we're going to rob his house for whatever and you're gonna help me. Plain and simple we improvise to get away clean, are your prints in a database? Because if you ain't, after this you best believe they'll be in one waiting for the day you get locked up. Unless you do exactly as I say."

"Nope. I'm sorry. I really am and it seemed like the thing to do at the time. Especially when I thought about the cop who shot me in the back. I'm sorry." She is about to cry and Pablo can't afford her to be breaking down at a crime scene.

"Look Rosa, it's cool. It's forgiven, water under the bridge. We can deal with this and trust we're okay. Thanks, you did the world a huge favor, I just hope you can live with it and not let it haunt you. Plus you can not tell a soul about this, not even Gloria. We will never, I mean never talk about it again."

"Alright. I hope I can live with it. If not I'll talk to you and I'm never ever going to tell a soul. Living or dead. Know what we are going to do? Just tell me, I'm at your command." She laughs as she says this last bit. He laughs with her thinking this bitch crazy.

"This may seem crazy, but after we search this muthafucka we are going to burn it so the evidence goes up and away. You take downstairs and I'll look up here, you see something like a safe let me know."

"Alright. I really am sorry for this predicament." Rosa walks out of the room and he watches her vanish down the stairs.

This situation might turn out alright and really after he breaks it down and analyzes the situation, Rosa did him a favor. That bitch got a lot of heart for slicing Benny open. Pablo thinking he got to give credit where credit was due. Don't twist nothing up, people murder for all type reasons. The thing is sending an officer of the law to the next life takes guts.

He looks around the room, it's one night stand with no drawers, just a single Tiffany lamp. There's two dressers, one behind him, the other is up against the wall to his right. To the left are the windows and the closet on that side. He starts opening drawers and tossing them to find nothing. Even moving the dresser to see if anything is hidden underneath and to look at the carpet for any different than it's supposed to be. He doesn't find shit.

When he looks under the bed it's a briefcase, he pulls it out. It has numbers on each side, but he'll pry it open downstairs. Setting it by the door, he goes to the closet and opens it to see it's a walk-in. Searching it and coming up empty-handed.

Pablo goes through the other rooms upstairs that turned out nothing. One was a kid's room so he didn't even mess with it. One was the bathroom and turned up nothing. When he gets downstairs he sits the briefcase down and looks for Rosa.

Pablo finds her in a room that looks to be a personal office. Everything is flipped and turned. "What'd you find Shawtie? I got a fucking briefcase. We'll bust it in the kitchen."

"I got a few things in the kitchen that I think are worth some money. The kitchen isn't really big either. Nothing was anywhere down here, we need to check the garage too."

They're both sweating like convicts at Sandy Ridge. They finish and head to the kitchen. It is small, a regular fridge, dishwasher, a sink, oven, microwave, and one table with six chairs around it. Nothing expensive, on the table is a few stacks of money, jewelry, and a set of keys. Pablo walks over to the table and sets the briefcase on top of it.

The money is 7 stacks of hundred dollar bills with the $10,000 band on them. There's three watches, 2 are Crystal Rolexes, one is a Tag Heuer. There's three diamond necklaces and a couple of tennis Diamond ankle bracelets. The keys are four on a ring and two have car symbols.

"Grab me a knife Shawtie. I wonder what these keys go to, it's not a lock box or nothing? It looks like a master key for a Master Lock, both except the smaller one. You ain't seen a lock?" Pablo asks.

Rosa hands him a butter knife, "Nope, let me go look around the rec room." She saunters out the kitchen as he pops open the briefcase is $40,000 in it in $100 bills and a note from none other than the infamous Mr. Tedwell. The note just says thanks and is signed by Tedwell. He decides to leave that alone for now, considering Benny no longer around. So there's no reason for him to talk to Tedwell. Actually he has things to sit on and analyze from the devil advocate view.

While he's standing there thinking to himself, asking where you would hide a safe or money that the average person wouldn't look. It's like a lightbulb going off as it slides across his mental forefront. Pablo rushes up to the rec room where Rosa is knocking on the walls.

"Rosa, where's that key? I think I know what it's for and it's not a master lock. Hurry up." Standing next to the video arcade game Rally X, next to it is the arcade Pac-Man. Rosa walks over and drops the small key into his hand. "Where are you going to try the key? I haven't seen anything that fits, not in here anyway." She pulls her hair back into a ponytail.

Not saying nothing he bends down in front of the arcade game and sure enough there's a keyhole as if it'd be on it in an arcade room and you open it for the change. Slide in the key and it's a perfect fit, turn it to the right and abracadabra. It's open. He pulls the lockbox door open revealing money in the hole, he reaches in and starts pulling it out.

He pulls out 8 stacks that are $100 bills in $10,000 bands. He uses the key on the Pac-Man and gets the same result. It's not a guess Rosa never saw this much money, cuz she was standing there with her mouth open. "Shawtie you better shut your mouth before something flies in it." They start laughing as they walk over to the pinball machines. Rosa follows after picking up the money from the carpet.

"Boy this is a lot of money! I'm thinking this robbing and killing shit I'm-"

"Get a hold of yourself! That's your adrenaline talking. This is a new time and you can't go spending money like crazy. That brings a lot of unwanted attention. So calm down." Pablo opens the first pinball machine.

"Okay. Sorry. You're used to this I'm not, sorry. I'mma calm down and I'll do exactly as you say. I'll do my best to heed your advice and not go spending crazy money."

Pablo tunes her ass straight out as he cleans out the 2 pinball machines. In one it was a bunch of photos in an envelope. The other one had a phone book in it with names. They go back to the kitchen and put everything in the briefcase except the photos. Opening the envelope soon as he looks at the picture his stomach flips. He holds his head down and doesn't let Rosa see not one flick. Putting them back in the envelope he tells Rosa, "Let's check the garage."

"What's up with those pictures? Why do you look pale as a ghost looking as if you are about to puke?"

"It's nothing, come on." Grabbing her hand and tugging gently to get her moving with him to the garage. When they get in the garage it is bare except for the lawn mower, a can of gasoline, and a weed eater. There's a door off to the left. They walk over to it and turn the knob it's locked.

"Rosa help me out here, find something to open the door without all the noise."

She smirks and pulls out the keys that were just on the table. "One of these a work. I saw the door early, excuse me." She walks up and goes 1 key at a time and the third key works unlocking it. "Bingo." She opens the door and its swings in and it's lit like the 4th of July in the room. "Rosa let me go first. Trust me." He pulls out the 9 and goes slowly into the room and down some steps. When he gets to the bottom it's like a sex dungeon. Pablo sees shit in this room that was in the pictures, only ain't no mutilated females.

Rosa puts her hand on his back, "What is this room? That sick fuck was going to probably try to drag me down here! Crazy muthafucka! I'm going to go back upstairs!" With that she goes like a light breeze on a summer day. Looking around and it's too much. Pablo sees nothing of importance so he leaves, back upstairs he grabs the gasoline can and walks in the kitchen.

"Rosa take the briefcase and get in the car. I'll be out in a few minutes."

"Alright. You sure you don't need my help with nothing else?" She picks up the briefcase.

"Nah. I got it from here." Snatching the pictures up and taking them upstairs and placing them on the nightstand, upright against the Tiffany lamp. He goes back to the kitchen and picks up the can of gasoline splashing on everything and leaves a trail out the door down to the stolen Lexus.

"Drive Shawtie." Rosa slides over into the driver's seat and starts the car up. Pablo tosses the can to the yard and bends down with the lighter.

Whoosh!

CHAPTER TWENTY-NINE

Pablo is sitting on the couch in Rosa's living room, while Gloria and her are in the back room talking. Only the Lord knows what they are talking about. He hopes it isn't about what just happened an hour ago. The surround sound they have is playing Twilight by Kevin Gates. He's smoking some lime green Kush that Gloria had on the dining table when they walked into the double-wide the sisters share.

He opened the briefcase and gave the two oyster Rolexes to Rosa who handed one to Gloria. So he knew what was up, so he handed each one of them a diamond necklace, and each a tennis Diamond ankle bracelet. Pablo also gave Rosa $130,000 and kept the other $130,000. That's when they got up and went into the back and he noticed the sticky and rolled up.

He already smoked one and is working on the second blunt, he's high as the sun at noontime. After he gets relaxed better on the couch he lets Gates' voice send him on a mental movie show.

Pablo still can't believe Rosa slit that muthafucka's throat or the pictures that he found. He was a cop/sicko, that bondage shit is crazy. A little is cool, but that shit he had a make any average person's stomach twist and turn. Pablo hopes that shit burned down before the fire department could put it out. At least her prints, because he knows shit going to fly. Even after they see the dungeon.

Rosa walks back into the living room sitting on the end of the couch relighting the blunt in the ashtray. "You high as fuck right now? Don't worry I didn't tell her anything except we robbed somebody. Gloria ain't going to say nothing, I promise. So you like this outfit?"

Pablo looks over at Rosa, she has on a tank top that shows off her big up right titties. Her nipples are dark and hard as a root beer candy. She is in a pair of red boy shorts that show her fat shaved pierced pussy. His mind is like don't, but his man in his pants rocks up and tents the polo jeans.

"I take that as a yes." Rosa smiles, putting the blunt out and strips naked.

"Shawtie, I'm warning you up front. I'm a bust a hole in your heart! Know what it is with me." He stripped naked faster than Usain Bolt running at the Olympics.

"Damn boy! Rosa says and doesn't waste no time, before she wraps her honey glossed lips around the dick. Shawtie moaning like crazy as he slides a finger in her wet tight pussy. She coming up and down bobbing faster and faster, gagging a few times. He pulls his finger from her dripping pussy and tells her, "Get up."

When she does he lays her on the floor and fills her oozing pussy all the way to the hilt. Pablo went slow at first then picked up his pace and Rosa moaned louder than the muthafucking surround sound. "Oh…yeah…give…it…to…me…I'm…cumming!" Bending her knees to her neck.

He starts to feel her pussy walls start doing a little squeeze and spasm that occurs when a bitch cumming. He's got her bent knees damn near behind her shoulders and is jackhammering the pussy like he's breaking concrete.

"Oh…Shit…I'm…About…To…Cum…Again…"

He feels himself about ready to bust a nut so he pulls out and lies on his back. "Let me bust this nut in your mouth."

Rosa sits up on her knees and leans over to swallow dick in her throat again. Her mouth game super like that. Soon as he feels himself ready to shoot he holds her by the back of her head and it went from blowjob to face fucking. Seconds later, cum explodes down her throat. She swallowed every drop like a good thot.

After she finished he lay there ready to go again. Rosa was ready as a hen in a henhouse. They fucked all over that double wide except in Gloria's room.

CHAPTER THIRTY

The line of mourners for Detective Benny Johnson's wake stretched outside the Hampton Funeral Home. Family and friends bid farewell Wednesday to the detective of 17 years. The detective was found murdered last Saturday in his home on Lake Catawaba. The house was partially burned down. The wake began as the Hickory-Lenoir native's murder was being investigated and the hunt for the ruthless killer or killers are sought. There is a $50,000 reward being offered for any information leading to an arrest. The detective's funeral is set for Friday at the Mount Helen Cemetery in Hickory.

Pablo tosses the News Topic down on the table inside Mc. D's where he's eating lunch. So far so good. Nobody can put Rosa and him at that scene. Except Rosa and she ain't gonna say nothing. He doubts it because Rosa a be done for like a pig over a spit.

He fucked the soul outta Rosa everyday this week and even got the dome from Gloria. She said she only lets her boyfriend hit the pussy. Pablo already told Rosa ain't no more, he ain't told

Bianca, fuck it. Bianca acting like her shit doesn't stink. That's the only reason he did it anyway.

He doesn't feel he did anything wrong about confronting her on that love shit. It's too much going on for him to be strictly one-on-one. Knowing one day when he is done with El Diablo then he'll fall back and be ready. Ain't no way he's gonna believe that he can't be booked for no major charge, that he is the one invisible to a casket 6 ft deep. You can't be doing wild ass shit and believe that for a second. If so and he thinks that, then he can sell a set of wings to a demon in hell.

Pablo still thinks every day about the coma he was laid in and the shit he dreamed. There's no way he can fully trust someone until he is done with killing pedophiles for El Diablo. Then the bullshit with BB, that in it itself could be a major blow back. He could be the one to get murked.

Bianca also has decided to let her situation that El Diablo gave her in that envelope go. She set it aside, out her thoughts. At least that's what she told Pablo when he brought it up at the studio the other day. Bianca is still the same inside and out, but she has done a 360 for the betterment of life. She's steadily marking days off the calendar for Pablo's day to quit.

He told her to give him until he was done with El Diablo and BB. He's not going to even worry about Archer. That's not a problem for real. The thing is to just do what he wanted to finish the time killing for El Diablo. Honestly he doesn't trust El Diablo at all, due to his name and number being in the phone book that he took from Benny's house. Plus the other situations from the past.

The number was disconnected, but still. It makes Pablo wonder and think some wild shit. He found out that the ones who got it be working with the police. Not all the time, but a lot goes on behind closed doors. Especially when someone has something dangerous to reveal about you or your loved ones.

Pablo disclosed all of the phone book with Alexis. She took a vacation to London and said they will talk when she gets back. To not get locked up, Pablo actually gave her no choice except to Vacation. BB finally told Pablo he's coming down for a couple weeks in a few weeks. He also said he's bringing a friend that he wants him to meet. Pablo can't wait to dust crop his brains all over the grass and the first isolated spot he gets a chance. Ain't no way he's leaving the city breathing.

For now he has to do a job for El Diablo later on and on the flipside, he doesn't even have to leave the city. The crazy thing is, it's like the closer Pablo gets to being done, El Diablo stepping up the murders. Pablo doesn't mind sending rapists, child molesters, straight-up predators to the next place on the soul's journey. It's that, having some of them actually got an innocent look in the eyes. Even to the end.

At the studio he Parks the AMG and strolls inside. Right now all three booths are being used. Gloria told Pablo this as he walked past the reception desk. He walks into his office and sees Bianca sitting behind the desk in the leather swivel chair.

The desk is an oak wood Kincaid desk. The walls are New York Giants blue on the left side. Duke Blue on the right. The wall behind the desk is with the Giants, Duke, NC State, Tarheel, Wake Forest, Notre Dame, Hornets, and Panthers logos.

There's two black swivel chairs in front of the desk. The door is solid redwood. On either side is a painting by a dude who calls himself Bodie Garcia. Underneath those on the left is a portrait of Tupac, on the right is a family portrait.

The carpet is navy blue with hints of gold scattered through-out. Stepping behind the desk and planting a soft kiss on Bianca's lips. They taste just like peaches.

"What's good Chica? You cool." Pablo pulls her up and sits her on his lap. She lays her head on his shoulder.

She has on a lime green Dolce & Gabbana dress with match-ing open toe heels showing off her size 5 pedicure toes. The pol-ish is lime green and on the big toe is a B&P in glitter. Her nails are manicured and painted lime green. She's rocking the diamond necklace and diamond tennis ankle bracelet that he gave her. Her face bears no make up as usual.

"I'm okay. Just been tired the last few days, more than usual. We need to talk, I mean oh, I need to clear the air about some things. Do you have time before you go check on the people in the booths?" She runs her fingers over Pablo's hand up one of his arms tracing the tattoos.

"Chica I always got time for you. You know that and it's some shit I need to get off my chest too. Go ahead and go first, I'll go when you finish." He kisses her lips slightly again. Now he understands what Bruno meant about kissing his girl all day.

Bianca sits up a little so she can look him in the eyes. "I know the last few weeks I've been kind of reserved. Somewhat sheltered and closed off when it comes to you. I'm sorry and hope you can forgive me. Usually I'm good at keeping my emotions under wraps and not letting them surface. The thing is with you, it's not possible at all, no matter how hard I try. I love you and did before I even slept with you. All I want is to be with you. Do you understand? I hope I'm not being too pushy."

Pablo takes a second to gather and get his words together before speaking. "Bianca I forgive you, not that you need it Chica. As long as you forgive me in the long run. Ain't no need to stress the love I have for your sexy ass. I fucked another bitch just to see if it change and it didn't. Now I'm not ever going to tell on my dick so don't ask, we cool so far?"

She nods her head and he's silent, still waiting so Bianca tells him, "It's cool, as long as you know I'll murk a bitch she gets outta line. I won't ask so it's like a military code. Don't ask, don't tell. We cool. I do have to say that I know you want Alexis. I do too, now you can finish."

"Chica, I wasn't expecting that. I don't know what Alexis a say, we got to talk to her. Now Chica, it's almost over with and I mean that. I gotta handle the situation today and I only owe a little more time to the cause. Plus a little demo about to be here from the kid up North. So I give you my word that when those two things are signed, sealed, and delivered I'mma hand you the one on one. Or one with two. We are going to take a vacation with the girls, consolidate all we got and live everyday together in total happiness." He kisses her again tasting the peach lip gloss.

Bianca looks as happy as a kid on Halloween. "You know I know when you give me your word it's solid and ain't going to break. I want to spend my life with you, ride or die, free or locked up, I'll be down for you and only you. I will never fold or crumble down on you. I want to help you with the girls, and give you more children. Preferably a son to carry your name and blood line. So I can wait this last couple months. My stuff is done too. Promise?"

"I give you my word, yours is done and over also. Long as it stays where it's supposed to and you know what I mean. I got you chica, and you ain't got to ever sweat me going to jail or prison again. As long as it's in my control. Hopefully that won't happen, I have too much out here for that to happen. I'm glad we are on the same page and let's always stay there okay?"

Bianca kisses him, "I got you Papi. No preocupación. Te amo mucho. Lock the door baby." He gets up and does just that.

CHAPTER THIRTY-ONE

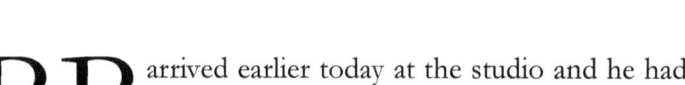

BB arrived earlier today at the studio and he had this chick with him who looks like a crackhead version of Lindsay Lohan. The chick perfume is too strong, her clothes too skimpy and shows off her bones, head to toe. Plus he can't get BB alone for one second, not that he'd blow his memories in the air of a studio.

"That shit was cold as ice in the South Pole! Now take it from the top Butter. Soon as the beat drop. You ready dawg?" Pablo in the booth and got the homie ButterStreetz on the phone. He's up at Central Prison and he is appealing his case, but in the meantime he is about to make his music known everywhere.

Pablo's brother Porno finally popped up from god-knows-where and he says he can do some beats before he gets ghost. The beat playing in the booth right now is a mix of old school Master P, the late style of Nate Dogg, and the new down south hard bass line soft trouble from DJ Khaled.

"Yeah. Start from the top, I gotta nail this verse before the phone goes off."

Pablo turns and twirls his hand in the air. And Porno takes it right to the top and drops a beat that knock a glass out of back windows.

"ButterStreetz always clutchin heat'- No defeat due to nobody able to compete/lay competitors under white sheets-Trigger finger faster than Usain at a track meet/Never sweet...cept in ur bitch mouth I skeet/Call me dreamcast makin' you part of da past/200 all gas like sega you don't last-tell your bitch I'm never half mast don't bust fast/Nobody like me...locked like me...free like me-breezy like me get dizzy like me/Never leaving niggas breathin' for no reason-it's ButterStreetz season a street heathen/Tuck bitches wit fat asses stack cash-Push foriegns two all on da dash/keep astash quick as flash-murder pussy niggas like I'm on M A S H]. There you go homie, the phone about to beep. Tweek it for me, I'mma get at you later my nigga. I'll call again in a few hours after count clear to hit the rest. Love to y'all."

The phone clicks off and Porno takes it back to the top so they can take out any background noise or distortions on the track. Then the vocals got to be inserted. This isn't as easy as Pablo thought. Pablo knows what it's like only to write and flow. Not the other aspects. He's learning through. "Porno I'm about to get out of here for a minute and handle some stuff. If I'm not back by the time ButterStreetz calls you can handle it right?"

"Yeah I got it and I'm a stick around for a couple weeks. Then it's some shit that needs to be taken care of. I've been on the move trying to get my name all the way out there. I'mma go see everybody later." Porno says.

"Alright I'm doing these beats that is gonna blast you in the stratosphere. I'm out, be easy." They dap each other up and Pablo walks to his office. Bianca sitting there and talking on the phone.

He lightly kisses her lips and whispers in her ear. "I'll be back in a few." She signals a hold on sign so he propped up on his desk.

"Okay. I'll be in next week then. No, that's okay, 2 p.m. Thank you."

She hangs up the phone. "We still going out tonight, Baby?" She stands up and puts her arms around his neck and he puts his hands on her bubble ass.

"Yeah Chica. I gotta handle this situation with the cat from up north. Then go see the old man after that and then swing back here. After that I'm all yours. Where are you trying to eat?"

"At J's cafeteria, you know they got the best food in Hickory. Plus I got a surprise for you, I believe you'll be excited. No, don't even think about it or try it, I'm not telling you till tonight. Now dama beso. Hurry back."

Pablo kisses Bianca for a few minutes and pulls back. Because he needs to evict these spirits back to the spiritual, while he has the attack of surprise on his side. "I'll be back ASAP Chica."

"Te amo." He doesn't reply as he walks out of the office door and stops at the entrance desk where Gloria is manning the station at the moment.

Gloria has on a pair of apple bottoms that look painted on her body. A white T-shirt with CRS on the front. "What's up Pablo? Before you ask, Rosa just stepped out for a minute."

"I'm not even trippin long as one of y'all sexy asses is here. I appreciate the rep for the studio on the shirt too. Have you got anything from the UPS man yet?"

"Nope. I'll give it to Bianca if you're not here. Ain't no big deal to rep the place I work. Oh yeah, tonight that country singer Eric Church wants to come record a song with the beat from Porno and verses from both y'all. I didn't interrupt when he called due to you talking to ButterStreetz in the booth."

"What time and ain't nothing free. I don't give a flying shit who he is or nothing, unless it helps the studio. That means helping all us eat and eat damn excellent. So no free shit."

Gloria shakes her head and tells him, "9 p.m. and he said it give the studio exposure to be featured on a song with him. Plus he said that y'all will talk about the rest yourselves." The phone rings and he takes that time to leave waving in the process.

CHAPTER THIRTY-TWO

Pablo pulls out Captain D's following his next victim. He takes a right onto 321 and then he takes a left on Finley Avenue. He's not right up against his bumper, just back far enough where you don't lose him. The target makes a turn into Holloway Projects, they're decent apartments and they're not like projects and other spots.

He watches Everett Davidson enter his apartment as he drives past. The apartments in Holloway have downstairs and upstairs on 4 of the buildings. The other two don't, they just single floors up and down. Pablo read the whole file El Diablo gathered for him on Everett. He is white, 5'5", 220 lbs going bald, out of shape, no job living off Social Security checks, divorced, no children, and been arrested twice for statutory rape. Once with a fifteen-year-old girl, the second one 13. Juries let him off both times.

Pablo makes a u-turn at the end of the street and parks four cars away from Everett's Accord. He decided to wait about an hour and then smash his brains out his cranium. The sweet thing is he doesn't gotta worry about nobody paying attention to him in the car he's sitting.

It's stolen for one, then the windows are tinted with mirror and he has put up the sunscreen and he's totally concealed. The windows are cracked just an inch so some cool air can get inside. It helps very little and in no time he feels the sweat rolling. Fuck this he's going now.

Pablo steps out the car and people are out, all races on the sidewalks, on stoops, pulling the Laker cap down further to shield his face more. It's 80 something degrees outside and it's 2:34 p.m. on his Walmart watch. He's as usual dressed in all black with Payless boots, black Goodwill pants, black shirt, and a black long-sleeve from super 10. He walks right up to Everett's door and knocks, rapping his knuckles four times and steps back.

Before he has to knock again Everett opens the door. He's standing there with a dingy white tank top, a pair of holy cargo shorts, and barefoot. "Can I help you?"

Pablo switches his voice to sound real proper and not street. "Mr. Davidson?" He looks kind of weary, "Yes."

"I'm from Blue Ridge Electric, I'm going to every apartment checking meters. People said that their boxes been given them problems. Have you had any difficulty, after paying money to be added to your box?" Pablo know some people have these boxes and he's flying off what El Diablo had in the file.

"I have the prepaid box, but I haven't had no problems. Knock on wood I don't, but you're more than welcome to check mine out. Come in and I'll show you where it's located." He turns around and Pablo steps in the apartment closing the door.

As soon as he takes a turn into the living room Pablo puts his fat, out-of-shape ass into the Charleston Chokehold and puts him to sleep without any problems.

He pulls out his phone from the wall and uses the cord to hog-tie him good and tight. He sweeps the apartment just to be sure he's alone. This muthafucka is a pack rat and nobody else is in the apartment. He's here for one reason and that reason is in the living room.

Pablo gets back and looks around the pitiful room. One couch, one recliner, an old ass TV hooked up with a DVD VCR combo box. He slips the green, yellow bandana in Everett's mouth. He hasn't used a color in Forever, he's using it because he's sending his soul to Santa Muerte in route to the devil. The yellow is for legal because he didn't want to use a yellow candle. Pablo slaps him awake.

After a couple smacks he's back fully alert. He starts trying to talk and it's just muffled noises. Pablo walks over to the TV and turns up the volume on the talk show. Walking back to Everett he gets a foot away, then starts kicking his left side as if attempting to send the left ribs through the right ribs.

"Aaaarg." Is all that is coming out and his wiggling isn't helping him at all. Tears are sliding down Everett's face to the dirty brown carpet beneath his hogtied body.

Pablo stopped kicking him and bends down, "That green and yellow flag is Santa Muerte color for legal problems, for justice. You have to stop in to her, before you meet the 3 headed guard dog on your way to the devil."

Pablo stands back up and walks on the opposite side and punches his right side as bad as he did the left. He stops and squats down again.

"You have any idea why I'm in your apartment? Beating the holy shit outta you. Shake your head yes or no."

He shakes his head rapidly no from side to side. Pablo gets up and walks around him twice just to mess with his head. He walks to stand in the little hallway for a minute and then walked back into the living room and swats down again.

"Everett, listen to me very well. Ain't no reason for me to sugarcoat nothing. You're going to die, I'm going to leave here breathing and you have to decide if you want it slow or quick. So when I ask a question, just answer truthfully. 'Cause answers I desperately need."

He nods his head and is trying to get words to come out through and around the gag. "I'm going to remove the gag, but if you so much as attempt to scream over the TV you getting no other chances. So don't be stupid."

He removes the gag which is covered in saliva so it's a good thing Pablo always wears gloves doing shit.

"Look, I don't know you or why you're-"

He cuts him off, "Save it for the Pope. Just answer my questions and you may change my mind about your whole situation. Don't lie either. Got it?"

Pablo confused him on purpose, because he just told him he's going to die.

"Yeah. I got it and whatever it is I'm telling you, I-"

"Stop or the gag goes back in and won't be removed again. Except by the cops or coroner. Now you got indicted by 2 grand juries on two separate occasions for charges correct?"

"Yes. I was charged with crimes that I didn't commit. That's why I was found not guilty. 12 people decided." He's pretty calm considering his situation right now. Pablo doesn't like that at all.

"How is it that two girls at two different occasions, two totally different cities, two different departments arrest you then? Explain to me how you, outta 150,000 fucking people, was the one handcuffed and set in jail a year one time and 18 months the next." Pablo punches him left, right, right. "Tell the truth."

Blood is trickling down his right eye onto the carpet. "Listen I'm telling you I don't know why I was picked up and charged. That shit ruined my life every way possible. My alibis both times were solid! Both times I was out of town on business. I-"

Smack! Smack! Smack!

"Quit the bullshit because it won't work! Now you are starting to piss me off and you ain't going to enjoy me pissed off! So quit lying!"

Smack! Smack! Smack!

He looks as if he's about to pass out so Pablo doesn't strike him again.

"Tell me how you got those girls to even let a pig like you do what you did and had to let the parents find out by their phones? Why did you do it when you had a wife? A grown woman."

"Man please stop hitting me, I'm telling you on my mother's grave that I never touched those girls! I had never seen either of them before I went to trial. I was set up and it's not a lie. The only thing they had was statements from those girls. My ex-wife is a looker, I wouldn't ever do what they accuse me of doing to those girls." His eyes are bleeding mixed with something else and he's either a good liar or somewhat truthful.

Pablo stands up, "Don't scream or say nothing until I get back." He steps back out of his sight in the hallway and leans against the wall and hears him praying. He blocks it out and is thinking about this whole situation. Something isn't exactly right or either he's just not scared enough.

Going into the little kitchen, opening drawers till he finds a knife that is sharp enough. Picking up the steak knife and going back to Everett and gags him again. "I told you not to lie and you keep doing it and on top of that you swear on your mother's grave! You're a real piece of work my man."

Pablo slices a 3-inch cut on his left cheek causing him to start going crazy with screaming through the gag. He then gives him a twin slice on the right cheek. Tears are mixing with blood, it's weird how blood and iron smell the same. It might be just him.

The blood flowing to the dirty brown carpet now in his eyes are begging like shit. Pablo waits a few minutes and removes the gag.

"Now explain the truth to me or gets a lot worse everywhere around we have to indulge in this knife tasting your flesh and blood."

"I swear to you on my mother's grave I didn't touch a single hair on those girls! Man, man, please stop this and let me live. I won't call the police. I hate the police and don't trust them considering how they falsely charged me and treated me like an animal. You got to believe me I never-"

The gag is back in his mouth.

Standing over him Pablo starts stabbing him all in his sides and back, like a convict putting in work on another convict. Fat muthafuckas bleed out a lot of plasma in blood. Blood is on his boots and pants and covering his right hand up to the elbow.

He stands back in front of him, he's almost ready to go out, he don't need that happening just yet. He removes the gag, "Truth or it's over for you now, no more fucking around!"

"Man... I... swear... I.. ne..ver... touched... those... girls... no.. under...age... girls. I'm... tell...ing... you... the... honest... 2... God... truth... same... as... I... told... de...tec... tive John...son... also..."

"Chill out, don't say nothing else. I'll be right back." Pablo goes searching for the bathroom and finds it at the end of the hall. He goes in and gets a couple towels, wets them down with cold water and heads back to the living room.

Bending down seeing the blood isn't leaking out as much, which he guess is good. He wraps the towels around Everett tight as possible, getting a grunt. Afterwards, he goes to get some water in a glass and lets him take sips.

"Listen, breathe easy and chill out. I'm going to untie you, don't make no stupid attempts to rush me or get away. If you so much as flinch wrong your adam's apple will be stuck on this knife after I feed you your own dick. Understand?"

"I...got you." He uses the knife to cut the phone cord off his wrists and ankles unhogtying him in the process. His legs and arms land on the bloody carpet and make a wet splashing sound. Something definitely wrong with this whole scenario. It's got Pablo confused as a Rubik's Cube being done for the first time.

He helped Everett put his back against the couch and ask him, "What does detective Johnson look like?"

He takes a couple breaths, "He was white...stocky...blonde hair...with...blue eyes...probably...6'2" or 6'...he was the... leading...invest...igator...both...times...why?" He lets him have some more water before he says anything.

There's a million thoughts zooming around the racetrack of Pablo's brain. If what he's thinking is true he wonders how many of the dudes might have been really innocent. He knows for sure without a doubt it could only be 2 innocent, counting out Everett. Knowing El Diablo's phone number, even being disconnected, was inside Benny's phone book is crazy. Really doesn't mean shit and then could mean a lot.

"Let me ask you something, how'd your name even come up? What I mean is if you never touched those girls then how'd your name end up in their phones?" Million-dollar question.

"Man…that's the…thing that…helped me get off…the…number…wasn't mine…it was to a woman in…a rest home…her number has…been the same…for…ever."

"Alright. Just chill for a minute, I'm about to get you some help."

Pablo walks into the hallway and pulls the throw away out his pocket, dialing a number he could recite in his sleep. After three rings it answered.

"Yo. Who's this?" BB asks.

Whispering into the phone so Everett doesn't hear him. "It's me, check it, I need your assistance on a legal issue. Can you ditch that bag of bones for about 45 minutes?"

"Yeah. Where you at? Do I need to bring anything more than my briefcase?" Pablo hears the chick that's a human walking skeleton in the background asking a million questions. "Shut the fuck up while I'm on the phone!"

"Nah. That's enough to handle the matter. I'm over where Tok hit Doobie up, third one on the left of Meka and DJ. Hurry up dawg."

He clicks the phone off walking back into the living room where Everett is semi-conscious.

"Sorry about this and I pray you a safe journey to whichever side that your spiritual path carries you on."

"I…thought…you said…-"

He cut him off, "You know that I can't do it, you've seen my face. If I let you go I'll have to not only watch out for po-po, but you also. Father in Heaven, mother in hell forgive me for the sin."

"I'm telling…-"

Pablo slices his neck with the smiley face and jumps back as artery blood squirts out. Damn, that shit ain't no joke.

CHAPTER THIRTY-THREE

Knock Knock. Knock Knock Knock. Knock knock.
It's been 30 minutes and BB just now arriving at the late Mr. Davidson's apartment. It's just about 5 p.m. so it will be dark soon and that's when Pablo will either make his getaway or be laying dead in this apartment.

He knows it's BB or someone he could have sent, which he highly doubts, because of the 2-3-2 knock on the door. That's what they used when showing up at each other's house or on a lick. He has another steak knife in his back pocket that he plans on using. Checking the peep hole, he sees BB standing by himself.

BB is dressed in all white which is dumber than shit. He's standing all 5'6", 160 pounds with his low fade fresh and acting like he is showing up to a photo shoot. Pablo opens the door and blocks himself from view just in case a nosey ass onlooker outside.

"Appreciate you coming dawg. Real talk." He watches BB close as he enters the hallway. Pablo really hates this is what their friendship came to.

"No problemo. Damn! Smells like a slaughterhouse in here already. How many people up in here?" He waves his hand in front of his face. Pablo shuts the door and points down the hallway, "One I murked in the living room. Two are tied in the room at the end of this Hall. I need help obtaining some info, so that's the reason I hit you up."

He starts heading down the hall, talking at the same time. "Ain't no thing, you know I'm a help you out any…" He gets out a choking sound as Pablo puts him in a Charleston chokehold.

"You done fucked yourself into a grave coming here! Pussy ass!" BB slams backwards taking them into the wall on the left, but Pablo doesn't let go as he continues choking him. He's going back again and Pablo swings around to the front so BB's face and part of his forearm meet the wall. Blood rushes out his nostrils. He starts scratching at Pablo's arms to no avail. A black long-sleeve shirt keeps the flesh intact, so it isn't ending up under BB's nails.

"Go to sleep!" He chokes him harder and he slammed into the wall again trying to get Pablo off his back and his arms from around his neck. Not a chance, today Pablo feeling lucky as a person spending their last quarter in the slot machine and winning big in Vegas.

Pablo can feel his body start to go lax and dropping down, so he goes down to the carpeted hallway with him. Holding on to BB until he sure his ass asleep. Only then does he let go and stand up. He takes the ripped up strips of the bedsheets out of his front pocket. Then ties him up really well, then drags him into the living room.

Pablo pulls his body through Everett's blood and drops him in front of the old brown recliner. This same dude he looked at as a brother. The same dude he ran the streets with. The same one that helped him fight in school hallways. The same one who helped them get money. The one he never would have thought would cross him for no one. The one he pledged loyalty with. Fuck this thinking, it's time to get done and out of here.

BB comes to and he stomps straight down on his face crushing his nose, bringing a bone breaking sound along with it. Blood is pouring like a water hose. He proceeds to stomp and kick BB up and down his whole body while he is letting out sounds of anguish. When Pablo finishes, he squats down with a steak knife in hand.

"Pablo man…why…you…doing this?" His voice is coming out sounding clogged up due to his nose.

"Bitch ass really going to lay bleeding in here and asking me why? You a certified burnout! You, the last mother effer I'd ever think or say, would cross me by harming me!" Pablo kicks him some more to his body, head and ribs breaking a few of them.

"Ah…ugh…ah…come…on…dawg…I..didn't…do…"

He places the same gag that was in Everett's mouth, that has saliva plus blood mixed on it into BB mouth silencing all talk and sounds coming from him. Knowing he can't really breathe now, well because the show is about to end for him, so time to roll the credits.

"Real quick I'mma explain, you started working for Archer to cross the old man. You knew he'd find out and more than likely send me to pay a visit. So you got Mario, Joey, and Carlos to help out when y'all wet my whip up in the Drive-Thru! I got hit up, but made it through with only more war wounds than before. Alejandra wasn't so lucky and died on the scene. I smoke them 3 amigos of yours and guess what? All three pointed at you and your own pops gave me the lowdown on everything! So now I finish all this and everything between us! Oh yeah, your bitch ass daddy is coming soon. ¡Contra toda mi amigos! You knew everything just like any other person!"

Pablo stabs BB over 30 times and that's just where he lost count. Before he stabbed the steak knife through both his eyes. Pablo is covered in blood, but that's a part of doing work. Be as silent as a ghost creeping through the night. Only tears don't come out of their eyes.

CHAPTER THIRTY-FOUR

Your honor, these charges are bogus. My client shouldn't be indicted!" Alexis is going back and forth with Jed Lake, the D.A. over his probable cause hearing for the robbery and gun charge. Alexis is standing all of her 6' plus a couple inches due to her Gucci heels. On her skinny frame is a Donna Karan dress that stops right above her knees. Her long black hair is wavy to the middle of her back.

Mr. Lake has on the common D.A. suit, he's around 5'5", 185 lbs mixed white and something else. "Due to detective Johnson being murdered your honor there has been problems. Problems that we were not able to solve in the 21 days we had before this hearing. We're asking that-"

"Your honor! With all respect for the court that isn't my client's problem! The arrest should have never happened in the first place! If the DA can not show cause to tie my client over to Supreme Court I ask this matter to be left alone."

Pablo is sitting there with no worries at all. Because Alexis has the proof of a plane ticket and airport camera to prove he wasn't even in Carolina at the time of the offenses. She's just trying to not show it in this probable cause hearing. Need be, she'll pop it to the Grand Jury today before they can indict.

"Mr. Lake I do not like my courtroom to be tied up or allow anyone to be paraded like a circus act. So now or never."

"No your honor, at this time the state cannot show enough evidence." Mr. Lake looks pitiful as he says this and starts gathering what little papers he has on the table.

"All charges are dismissed without probable cause! Next case will be heard in 10 minutes! State versus Wiseman!"

Alexis and Pablo head out the courtroom and don't stop until they're at their respective cars. Pablo is in his 92 Celica that has the 19 inch racing tires attached to Victory racing orange rims. He had the paint job redid in a Tony the Tiger mural.

Alexis throws her briefcase into the front seat of her Porsche 911 Targa 4 GTS 2015. She has the top open, it's cherry red with the rims and wheels still Factory. "Please try to stay out of trouble. You got lucky this time Pablo, next time I can't say because you are doing crazy shit. For the life of me I don't understand or know why. "She leans against the 911. "You're going to give me an early grave. Why not let's all just leave?"

He leans against the Celica dressed in Polo jeans, black forces, and a button Carolina blue polo shirt. No jewelry, fresh shape up with low fade. He doesn't ever expect Alexis to understand, but she good people from way back when he was growing up. Chica just took a good path and made some out of her life. Not that he hasn't, he just went a different route. She the one other person truly know why he's doing this.

"Look Alexis, you have known me half my life right? So you know how I'm going to be and what I do. No, I don't expect you to ever understand, nor even agree on any level. Because you're a law-abiding citizen, but I'm almost done with it all. A few more months and I'm going to be just like you. An honest tax paying citizen raising my daughters. Have you talk to Bianca?"

"No, not yet. I have another case to prepare for. Let me ask you something Pablo. You say you don't lie to me and never have right?" Alexis knows this, but asks anyway.

"Right. You are not just my lawyer, you are my people's, same light as wifey." He has no idea where she could go with this conversation.

Alexis eyes are honey brown that can put anyone in a trance or drown you into a sexual abyss.

She points her finger at him, "Tu cambio, from good to worse to good to worser to-"

"Worser is not a word, Chica." He smirks knowing she doesn't like being interrupted when she's talking.

"You know exactly what I'm saying, don't be funny here! I've seen you doing what was needed and the last two years it's as if you're psycho! Change for the worse to the point of no return. I don't want to come to your funeral or witness your life get thrown into prison! What good will it do for any of us? Stop while you're ahead."

"Alexis I'm telling you that neither is going to happen any time soon. Chica I remember what that cell was like and it ain't happening again. I got the studio, I got money put up, I only got a few months left to do wet work and I'm done. Don't forget you ain't always been an angel with your sexy ass."

"Nobody said I was, but I changed because of what happened that night and haven't looked back since. You may find this hard to believe, but every dime you've given me the last four years is still in the bank. Why? Because I would defend you in any court for nothing. Don't forget they can and will lock your ass up on bogus charges. I know you can't see yet, you know what it is here." She points to her heart, he knows this without a doubt.

Just as he knows what night she's talking about and it wasn't good. That was the first time he ever laid a soul to rest. That isn't something a person forgets no matter how cold their heart is.

"Why do you keep the money? I told you to spend it, because if I ever had it you would too!" He raises up off the car.

"You know how I feel and I know what I have to do to be content and happy and everyone else. I don't need to spend it for one. I have a lot of money because of you, I live simple. Not looking at the car or house and I remember you telling me that. All I'm saying is just lay back as soon as possible because nothing lasts forever. We know that better than anyone in our circle. Plus if that ever happened again-"

"Yeah. Look, I respect you and all you do and I'm proud of you. It is almost over, I promise. You want to get some lunch or you have another court appearance." Pablo asks. "Plus I got to upload my findings to you." "Where did you have in mind? I have a few hours in the window before my next appointment." Alexis looks at her Bolivia watch.

"How about Hams up in Hickory?" He starts to get in his car knowing she'll follow. They used to eat there when they only had lint in their pockets running out before they could stop them. No matter how many times they did that, people still serve them food. Once they got some money they fixed the tab.

"Okay. Don't get any ideas, yet." In his mind the idea never got evicted.

CHAPTER THIRTY-FIVE

Pablo is sitting on his back deck smoking a Philly filled with some peach widow. Bianca and his daughters are asleep inside, he's sitting on the steps leading to 3 acres of backyard that's fenced in by a 10 ft tall wooden fence. The backyard is a mini Park that his daughters, nephews can't get enough of when they're at the house. He only has on Nike Slides, a pair of Under Armour shorts. He's letting the cool night air caress his skin. That's a little thing he missed while being locked up, he couldn't be out at 2 a.m. looking at the stars feeling the air. The Earth we live on is majestic, so now he tries to suck in as much as possible. Like sitting out here in Tranquility thinking about past, present, and future.

Right now as he inhales letting the smoke fill his lungs he's in the past. Way back to be exact. 14 years ago on a night that was a lot just like this one. Only difference was he was 14, wild as shit, fresh out of juvie hall, chilling with Alexis...

"Boy am I happy to see you home!" Alexis runs to hug Pablo when he walks up with BB. 2 hours before he got picked up from juvie after doing 23 days for assault with intent. The charge got knocked down to aggravated battery, the judge put him on an ankle bracelet. He cut it off as soon as he got home, fuck wearing a tracking device like an animal.

"Chica don't knock me over! Crashing into me like you a bowling ball. Dama beso!" He kisses Alexis and grabs her butt. "You miss Papi ain't it?" He steps back.

"Yes! What time do you got to be inside?" Alexis holding on to his hand swinging their hands as girls enjoy doing when they feel puppy love.

"Whenever. I do what I want Chica, you know that. Parents ain't trippin, they are getting high as usual. BB I'ma catch you later."

"Alright. I know what you have on your mind. I'll be at princess' house." They dap each other and BB struts down Garnet Avenue.

He kisses Alexis again and they start walking in the opposite direction headed towards her house. Because her stepdad and Mom get high like 99% of their friends' parents. The difference is Alexis's mom lets them chill in her room and doesn't care what they do.

"So what was it like? Did you fight a lot? How are the police there? You wrote a lot, but never told me any of that."

Alexis has on a pair of sandals showing off her pretty toes, pink daisy dukes, pink halter top. He's rocking Bugle Boy and a white tee with a pair of Air Max. Thinking how he can't wait to start making money off the hustles picked up in juvie. That's a teenage school for criminology.

"Chica it was like school, just all boys from 11 to 18. I had to fight the first day, but it wasn't nothing. You know I hold on all levels. The COs ain't really fuck with us. I miss the fuck out of you!" Kissing her again, not stopping a step.

"Your name ain't no Dice to me. You're Pablo Valdez. Play that nickname shit with BB in them. Have you ate yet?" They're walking up her dirt driveway that leads to her house. It's a two bedroom that reeks all the time of crack smoke. The only difference is his peeps only smoke in their room trying to hide it. She's an only child and her room is the best smelling place.

"Whatever bubble butt! I don't want anything, I ain't hungry for real. Let's just get up in there so we can handle business!" She playfully punches his arm.

"That's all you think of! What if we just stopped, then what?" They step in her house and pass her mom, step dad and like five others getting high. They don't even give second thought to it for a second or glance at the glass dicks in their mouths.

They step in Alexis's room and she locks the door as he sits on the old hand-me-down bed. It's the box spring and mattress with nothing but the floor underneath. It's stuffed animals and clothes everywhere. Most of her clothes and shoes Alexis has stolen. She has posters of the greatest Latina singer ever, life taken short by Jealousy. Queen Selena.

Alexis sits next to him and pulls out her stash of weed. They get high as a bird in the clouds listening to H-Town. After he bust her back out they fall asleep for they don't know how long before her bedroom door crashes open. Pablo automatically grabs the 38 snub nose off the floor.

Her mom's boyfriend is standing there breathing hard as hell like he just ran a marathon. "What the fuck that about holmes? You better step back!" Pablo sits up and starts putting on his clothes.

"Get out of here! Are you loco breaking my door! Mama!" Alexis is covered by the blanket yelling at the top of her lungs. Pablo can hear her mom crying in the little house.

"Oya Princesa! Tu sobre you're going to be up in my house if in some no bueno Chico without my say so? You either pay me money or dame cabeza!" He starts into the room.

Pablo is sliding his shoes on when Alexis goes in rapid Spanish and asking him if he is crazy and she would never sleep with him and screaming for him to get out from her room. Just as Pablo is getting up to handle the situation he knocks him clear off his feet, the gun dropping. He starts raining fist on him talking about how Pablo is going to watch what he does to Alexis's little hot ass. Alexis jumps back covering his head with the blanket and it's just enough time for him to get his hand back on the 38 snub nose. He points and lets loose all six bullets. He drops to the floor and Alexis let's go of the blanket and him falling back on the bed.

"Midios Pablo! Midos! I can't believe you-"Alexis is freaking out hella bad so he covers her mouth with his hand.

"Calmate Chica! Por favor! Calmate! It's cool, it's gonna be alright! Trust me!" He removes his hand from her mouth.

Tears are cascading down her face. "Pablo I didn't mean for you to kill him! Oh my God! You're going- get out of here now! Give me the pistol. Now!"

That ain't likely going to happen. He'll see Moses tablet before the gun goes in her hand. He shakes his head, "Get dressed, Chica, now! Only touch your clothes."

Putting the gun in his waistband and checking to see if the old boy got a pulse. They flipped him over and his pulse is barely visible, "Fuck this piece of shit. Come on, we gotta check on your mom. He grabs Alexis's hand and speed walks into the living room. It's empty. Shit!"

"She's in her room, come on Pablo give me the-"

"Shut the fuck up Chica! You are not getting this gun under any circumstances! I don't give an f about that slimeball in there, he just disrespected you and got dealt with! Let's make sure your mom's good!"

"I don't want you getting locked up. Baby I'm a woman and the cops won't arrest me because of what happened. The door is proof let's-"

"Chica quit talking! I mean it, I'm not playing right now!" Pablo pushes open her mother's bedroom door, "Holy shit!" He pushes Alexis back. "Stay out there chica!"

She bursts in anyway and loses it for real. She collapses on the bedroom floor where her mom is curled up in the fetal position bloody as hell crying. Pablo dips out the room and comes back with wet towels and cleans her mom up best as possible. But Alexis is talking to her mom rapid in Spanish. Pablo can't follow what all is being said, it's too fast. Then Alexis tells him, "Pablo, baby. Please go and let us handle it. Even my mother says for you to leave. I'll see you tomorrow." He hesitates and then hauls ass out of there.

Damn that was a long time ago and yet it still feels like it was yesterday. He didn't see Alexis again after that night for three and a half years. They lied to the police about what happened and left the city to live out in the midwest with her grandmother. He went to juvie prison for 18 months later for two years and when he was released, Alexis was at Pablo's welcome home party.

Alexis and Pablo tried to pick up where they had left off, but it just didn't work. So they just remained friends and only three of them ever knew the real story about who killed her stepdad. Her mom passed away the day after Alexis graduated from Law School.

Today was the first time they've ever hinted around the subject of that night. Alexis feels as if she owes him, she doesn't owe him jack shit. If anyone owes anybody at all, it's him. Pablo owes her for getting her mother to cover up what happened because he knows how it would have ended up for him.

Alexis was the first true love and he prayed to every deity that he ever heard of that their relationship would work. It just wasn't in the cards. Life's a bitch. Yet here he is trying to change that bitch called life.

Pablo gets up and walks in the house peeping in at his daughter sleeping. He stands there for a few minutes before he heads back to bed with Bianca. She's still knocked out sleeping hard as a rock. He slides back into the bed and pulls Bianca's body closer to his body. She mumbles and scoots her ass back against him. "What time is it, baby?"

"It's almost 4:30, I didn't mean to wake you up Chica. Go back to sleep." She rolls over to face him and with morning breath and all.

"Pablo, we need to talk. I didn't- you didn't give me a chance last night after you put the princesses to bed." Bianca is all the way awake.

"What's up? It must be important if you are going to tell me at 4:30 in the morning with that atomic fire breath!"

She pushes him playfully and sits straight up while he's laughing and is given a full view of her nakedness as she straddles him. "You want some more of this dick!"

"Alright now! I'm being serious right now, so listen to me and no I didn't plan for this to happen. It just did so don't think nothing crazy or stupid and I'll do whatever you want."

"Shawtie just spit it out, it can't be that bad so stop doing all this beating around the bush." He playfully smacks her ass cheeks making them bounce.

Bianca takes a breath and then rubs her belly pointing. She has a joy in her eyes and he knows exactly what she's telling him at that moment.

"You for real Chica? I thought you were on the morning-after pill or something."

"If you remember at the studio that morning, I'm 7 weeks in and I want nothing more than to give you another child. I promise I will never be like Rebecca. You know-"

"Shh. Dama beso." She leans down and he kisses her, easing any and all fear she may or may not have. As he rolls over to be on top of Bianca he hears Dixie going crazy. Next he hears a loud crash, flash bangs, and off instinct he keeps moving to reach under his pillow. Muthafuckas have to be off their rockers to break into his house. This ain't for a pistol, this is Draco time he thinks as he can hear his daughter screaming. Before he can get off the bed the bedroom door comes flying off of its hinges. Before he knows it he slammed face-first to the bedroom floor and hears, "secure one!"

"Two secure!"

"Three secure!"

"Four secure!"

"Five secure!"

"All clear out front!"

"The back is clear."

Pablo can feel the steel tightening on his wrists and starts going off like a crazed man. Bianca get to my girls! Catch Alexis! You know how to handle the rest! You! Pussy ass muthafuckas!

Not! One! Fucking! Hair! Better! Be! Moved! On! My! Daughter's! Heads! I'll! Kill! Everyone! Of! You! Tu! Es! Familia-!"

"Mr. Valdez, your daughters are shaken up, but fine, we'll allow your spouse to go to them. You-"

"Muthafuck you bitch! You pussy-" Something placed over his mouth and he realizes it's a piece used to keep you quiet. Or in the system from biting or spitting on C.O.s. They dress him with boxers, and that is it. They lead him out of the house and escort him to the back seat of the nearest squad car. He is sitting there for about 10 minutes and rolls up a news van. Then the impossible, well not all the way impossible. Yet Alexis nor him could or would have ever thought of this outcome. He's thinking at the same time as they lock eyes, this was supposed to be handled in the field. In the war.

A couple black-clad officers walked over and one asked, "Is this the man who killed your son Mister Vega?"

Pablo looks right into the eyes of his Pop's murderer as he answers the officer. "Yes sir. This is him officer, he's the perpetrator." El Diablo winks as he walks off.

Oh no, this is not Checkmate El Diablo, this is to finally expose you for the snake you truly are. Pablo made a vow at 10 that he will uphold no matter what. Rico 'El Diablo' Vega will not make his next birthday even if I die in the process Pablo tells himself.